SOMEDAY BEACH

THE GRAYTON SERIES

JILL SANDERS

GRAYTON

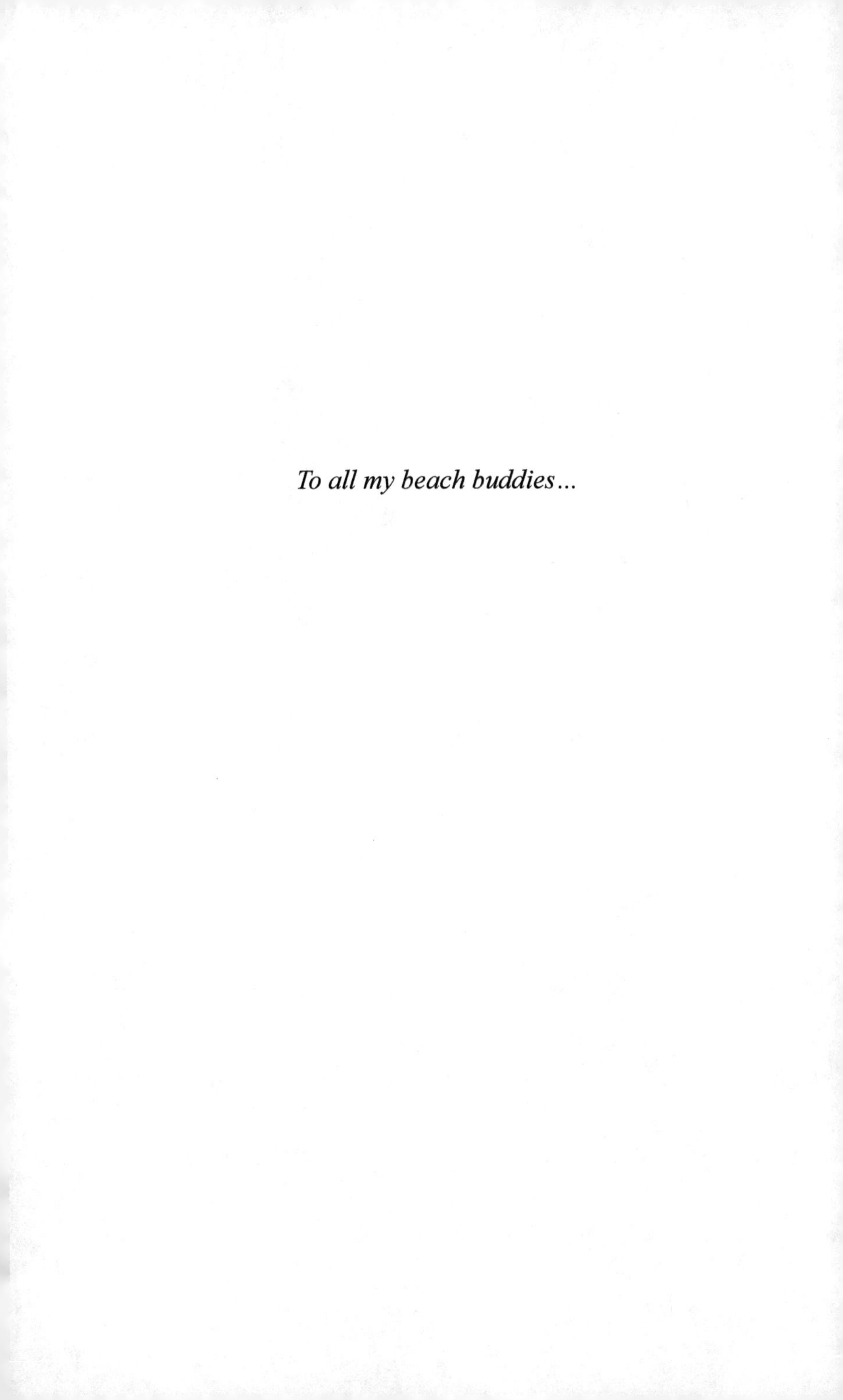

To all my beach buddies...

SUMMARY

Shelly has always dreamed of going back to Surf Breeze. When she finally sets out on her own and buys a rundown building along the popular boardwalk, she hires a sexy contractor to help her turn it into her dream boutique. But she hadn't counted on slowly changing with her surroundings. Fighting against an overbearing family, she learns to not only follow her own dreams but to stand up for something she believes in.

Marcus has been waiting his whole life for a woman who could see through the horrors he'd been through as a child and the humor he uses to mask it all. Now that he's found her, he's not quite sure what comes next.

*H*is whole body throbbed. Closing his eyes only made him think more about the pain, so he kept his eyes focused straight ahead of him in the dark. He could hear cars zip by outside his window on the free-way, which was only a few feet from his back patio. The small two-bedroom apartment was on the ground floor, and everything shook whenever a semi went by too fast.

When he heard a noise, he hoped it wasn't Mike, his mother's latest boyfriend, moving around in the next room. He squeezed his eyes shut and prayed that his mother would come home from the bar soon.

When he didn't hear anything for what seemed like an eternity, he chanced opening his eyes to glance at his Batman alarm clock. Its yellow numbers read one a.m.

He knew that the bar was just closing now, but since his mother was making extra money on the side by danc-ing, she wouldn't be home for at least another hour. Which meant that it *was* Mike moving around.

Squeezing his eyes closed one more time, he prayed

again that the man had gotten his fill a few hours ago. His six-year-old body began to shake when he heard his bedroom door open slowly.

Wrapping his little fingers around his protection, he prayed that this time he'd have the guts to use it against the bigger man. When Mike had woken him up for the first time that night, he'd been dead asleep and had forgotten all about his plan to rid himself of the horror that he'd lived through over the last eight months.

His heart stopped when he heard the floorboard next to his bed creak and he took a deep breath. Not giving himself enough time to question his actions, he lunged from his bed. Mike had only enough time to see the gleam of the fillet knife as it arched downwards towards his heart.

ne year later…

Marcus glared at the big house as the car bumped up the dirt road. The place looked like monsters lived there. Half of the shingles on the roof were a different color than the rest. The siding on the massive place had been sanded down to the bone by the wind, and some of the boards needed replacing. The front porch was caving in and when he leaned up a little, he could see that the front yard was a jungle of green that needed to be clipped, or better yet, burned. For that matter, the whole place should be torn down.

"You can't be serious!" He turned to the pretty blonde woman he'd come to know only as Lilly. She'd shown up at the boys' home a few weeks ago. At first, all the guys had whistled at her and made crude comments. All of them, except Marcus. Maybe that's why she'd taken an interest in him at first.

She'd asked Mr. Everette, the head of New Hope Boys' Home if she could meet with him. It had been just over a year since his mother had dropped him off at the front door of the home for troubled boys. A little over a year since he'd tried to kill a man, defending himself. Of course, his mother hadn't believed his side of the story, nor had she called the police that night. Mike had a few outstanding warrants against him.

Instead, she'd stitched up the large gashes on his shoulder and neck herself. When she caught him stashing another knife under his pillow that next week, it had taken her less than an hour to abandon her son.

Good riddance. Now he was a ward of the state and he liked it that way. Glancing over at the blonde again, he frowned and crossed his arms over his chest to make his point clear.

Lilly just smiled back at him as she stopped her car at the end of the drive. "The old place could use some work, but you're going to like the Graytons." She reached over and patted him on the shoulder. He didn't jump at her touch, nor did he flinch. Women didn't bother him much.

He leaned forward and looked at the house again. "Don't they have any money? I mean, sheesh." He shook his head. "If you have a house that big, ain't you supposed to be rich?"

"Aren't," she corrected him. She smiled over at him and then leaned forward and looked at the house herself. "Mark and Elizabeth have two daughters, Karen and Julie. They're older and only Julie lives at home still." She glanced over at him. "They could use someone like you around the house."

He frowned a little. "Like me?"

She chuckled. "Mr. Everette has told me that you have a talent with building and fixing things."

He shrugged his shoulders when she didn't continue. "I guess I like tools." He thought about all the birdhouses he'd made over the last few months. He was getting better at making them, faster too.

"Well, I figured we could try this out. You know, get you out of the city. Just look around here." She quickly opened her door and got out. He followed her a little more slowly.

When the fresh spring air hit him in the face, he closed his eyes. He'd never felt or smelled anything so wonderful. He could hear birds chirping in the tall trees that surrounded the old house. Looking up to the sky, he marveled at how blue it was. Living in the dirtiest part of Miami hadn't allowed him to really appreciate the sky.

Lilly walked towards the house, but he didn't want to follow her. Instead, he looked around some more and spotted a large three-car garage near the back of the house. When he walked towards it, he noticed an old band saw and table saw were sitting right out in the open.

"Here they are now," Lilly said behind him, causing him to stop. When he turned around, he saw three people walk out onto the old front porch. They all looked at him with huge smiles on their faces. He'd never seen people so happy to meet a complete stranger before.

There were two women. One was older and much larger than the other. The younger one had short, curly brown hair that was pulled back from her tan face by a bright scarf. She had a soft face and kind eyes.

Then an older man stepped forward. He looked so frail that Marcus no longer wondered why he had let the place go. The old man looked like he could barely walk down the stairs, let alone get up on a ladder and paint. He doubted he'd have a hard time fighting this guy off if he ended up being anything like Mike. But something in the man's eyes told Marcus he wasn't in danger here. Still, it was better to be cautious, at least for a while.

"Well, hello," the old man called out as he waved to them.

Lilly walked over to Marcus and took his hand in hers, then knelt down in front of him until they were eye to eye. "If you don't like it here, all you have to do is call me, and I'll come take you back to New Hope. Okay?"

He nodded and then looked over to the three people, who looked more nervous than he did.

It took him precisely two days to decide that he never wanted to leave the Graytons. Two days of Mr. Grayton teaching him how to use all the tools in the massive garage. The man had even told him that he could build anything he wanted. All he had to do was ask and they would have the materials delivered from the local hardware store.

Two weeks later, he'd sanded and replaced a lot of the siding on the old house. He didn't want to stop there, so he asked Mr. Grayton if he could fix the porch.

The old man had sat in his chair and scratched his chin. At first, Marcus had thought he was going to say no.

"Don't you want to run around and play like other kids do, instead of work?"

He frowned a little. "No, I like fixing things." He looked down at his hands, noticing the calluses that he'd earned from hard work.

"It's up to you. You're free to do whatever you want." Mr. Grayton had chuckled. "I'll have the lumberyard deliver the wood as soon as they can."

"I've…" He pulled out a piece of paper. "I've got a list here." He handed it over to him.

Mr. Grayton looked at it and frowned as he read the long list.

"You put this together?" He looked up at Marcus. When Marcus just nodded, he watched a smile creep onto Mr. Grayton's face.

"You have a talent for sure." He laughed. "Damned if I'm going to stand in your way. Why don't we ride into town tomorrow and you can show this to Jim down at the lumber mill yourself?" He handed the material list back to Marcus.

It had taken Julie, Mark, and him a whole month to finish the new porch. Julie was strong for a woman. She said she enjoyed wearing overalls and getting her hands dirty. Mr. Grayton had insisted that Marcus call him Mark.

He quickly came to realize that the old man wasn't as frail as he looked. He carried most of the heavy wood up to the porch and had even helped hold the new supports in place while he'd screwed them in. When all the work was done, they had painted the entire thing. Even Mrs. Grayton had come out of the house to help.

The day after all the paint was finally dry, he stood outside admiring his handiwork. He turned when he heard a car drive up the long drive and frowned when he saw that it was Lilly's car. His heart skipped a beat. The first thing that flashed into his mind was that she was here to take him back to the home. Maybe the Graytons hadn't liked him? Maybe he'd done something wrong?

Lilly stepped out of the car and waved at him. Her smile caused his heart to slow a little. She didn't look like she was here with bad news. Then a boy around his age stepped out of her car. The dark-haired boy looked a lot like he did except for the black eye and broken nose. His left arm was in a thick white cast and he walked with a slight limp.

Lilly rushed over and helped the boy walk towards the house. "Good morning, Marcus. Are Mark and Elizabeth home?"

He shook his head no. "They went into town to pay the water bill." Lilly and the boy walked up the stairs he'd just finished painting the day before.

"Wow! Doesn't this look wonderful?" She exclaimed. Then she did a quick turn, looking at everything. "Did you do all this?"

Marcus nodded, not taking his eyes off the boy, who was staring at him like he was going to rush across the new porch and punch him.

"Is Julie home?" Lilly turned back towards him.

Marcus nodded again. "She's inside making sandwiches."

"I'll just let myself in. This is Roman." She turned back towards Marcus, holding the screen door open as she looked at him. "If everything works out, he'll be staying with you here for a while." She smiled at them both, then turned and disappeared into the house.

"How'd you break your arm?" Marcus asked.

Roman looked down and shrugged his shoulders. His

brown eyes had opened wide when Marcus had talked to him, and he figured the kid was scared to death.

He could remember a time not so long ago that he'd felt that way. Walking over, he stood in the corner of the porch and sighed. "It needs a swing, doesn't it?" He waited and when he didn't get a response, he turned back towards Roman.

The kid was staring at his shoes like it was the most important thing in the world.

"Right here." He motioned to the spot just below the front windows. "Maybe I can hang some chains from those beams there." He nodded above him and tilted his head sideways. Out of the corner of his eyes, he saw Roman look up at the ceiling of the porch.

"Maybe some planters?" He folded his hand and rested his chin on his fingers, much like he'd seen Mr. Grayton do when he thought about what Marcus had suggested. "Course, planters could go here." He motioned to the windowsills. "Or here." He walked over to the railings he and Mr. Grayton had finished putting up a few days ago. Really, it was Julie who had helped the most. But Mr. Grayton had sat on his stool and helped Marcus place each rung in the railing himself.

Marcus couldn't ever remember laughing or having such a good time with a man before. Mark Grayton was a joker. Marcus could never really tell when he was being serious or pulling his leg. He loved every moment of it and wanted to be just like the man when he grew up.

"Your yard needs mowing," Roman said from behind him. His voice was small and, at first, Marcus questioned whether he'd heard correctly.

Turning he smiled at him. "What it needs is a few

dozen goats." He chuckled. "Do you know, I was walking to the pond the other day and got lost in it." He laughed at his own joke.

He thought for a moment he saw a slight smile on Roman's face. "So, do you think you'd want to help me build some flower boxes and mow the grass? I mean after your arm is all better?"

Roman glanced down at his arm again. Marcus thought he wasn't going to answer, but then his dark head nodded. "I suppose."

"Good." He smiled and walked over and held out his hand. "I'm Marcus… I have a feeling we're going to get along just great."

That night, he lay in his big bed and listened to Roman cry in his sleep. He knew it wouldn't do any good to go to the kid. It had taken him almost seven months to stop crying about what he'd gone through.

The least he could do was keep the kid busy over the next few months, to keep his mind off of his pain.

That summer, Roman and he became best friends. They were inseparable. Roman had a good eye for some of the finishing touches that Marcus didn't have the patience for. Together they finished the swing and flower boxes and built over a dozen colorful birdhouses that they hung in trees all over the property. They had even built one that looked like the big house itself. It hung off the front porch in a place of honor.

Less than two months later, they watched Lilly's car drive up again. This time, it was a little blond boy that stepped out. He didn't have a broken arm or a scared look in his eyes.

It had taken less than a week for Roman and Marcus to accept him. Julie had taken them to the beach one day, and they'd sat in the sand watching Cole bodyboard. Marcus had never seen anyone do flips like that in the water before. It was like the kid was part dolphin and that had earned him all the respect he'd needed to be part of the family.

Over the next few years, Lilly's car would come only two more times. These times, instead of boys, she'd delivered girls.

Marissa was first; she was very small and had short blonde braids. Even though she was tiny, she sure knew how to boss all three boys around.

The next month, Lilly's car came up the driveway and a dark-haired girl climbed out slowly. Marcus had known without a doubt that she'd gone through something far worse than any of them had. She was so skinny, he thought the wind would knock her over.

Instantly, Marissa had taken Cassey under her wing. By the end of that next year, the Graytons made it official and formally adopted every one of them.

That evening, after signing papers at the courthouse, the five of them stood out by the pond and made a promise to one another that nothing would ever break up their new family.

CHAPTER 2

*S*eventeen years later…

Shelly stood back and dusted off her hands. There was a slight splinter in her thumb, which she would have to deal with later. Her clothes were covered in dust and she was sure her hair and face were as well. It had taken her almost three hours to clear out the room she would be using as a bedroom for the next few weeks. At least she hoped it was only going to be for a few weeks.

She frowned a little thinking of all the work that needed to be done as she looked around the place. Then she smiled, realizing it was all hers. She sighed and rubbed her hands together. Well, she wasn't going to get anything done just standing around.

Rushing from the room, she grabbed her keys and headed downstairs to start bringing boxes up from her car.

When she opened the outside doors, the cold salt air hit

her in the face and she smiled. It was going to take some getting used to, living by the water.

She chuckled as she unlocked her car and started pulling out the first load of boxes. She'd always dreamed about living near the ocean, of falling asleep to the sound of the waves or waking up and seeing the seagulls fly overhead.

The back stairs to her new place were wide, allowing her to carry the large boxes up easily, even though they weighed more than she wanted to lift. Her back was going to kill her tomorrow. She frowned and shook her head. It was a price she was willing to pay.

It took her less than an hour to get all the boxes from the back of her Jeep and the small U-Haul trailer she'd rented.

When she was done bringing up the last box, she rinsed her face off and brushed her hair. Grabbing her purse, she stepped out onto the boardwalk just as the sun was sinking over the water.

Even though her stomach had been growling at her for the last hour, she took her time and watched in amazement as the sky filled with bright colors. Couples walked hand in hand along the sandy shore. She sighed and felt like spinning in circles of joy. She'd finally made it here. To her someday beach.

Even though the crisp air screamed winter, she didn't mind. She watched as all the lights turned on along the long walkway.

There were over a dozen stores, restaurants, and other business along the boardwalk, and if she had anything to say about it, she was going to be one of them in just a few short months.

Turning away from the darkening sky, she headed back towards the buildings and smiled up at hers. It was one of the most damaged, yet it stood out like a beacon in the night. Its bright white stucco walls and mirrored windows caught the dying light. She could see every crack, every broken window, even though the lights were off.

Her stomach growled loudly as a couple walked by her. Putting her thoughts and dreams aside, she headed down to the restaurant along the boardwalk.

When she stopped in front of the Boardwalk Bar and Grill, the wonderful scents of food hit her and made her realize she was a lot hungrier than she'd thought.

Even though it wasn't high-season, the place was packed. For a moment, she wondered if she'd be better off going somewhere else.

Then a dark-haired woman smiled at her and showed her to a small table near the windows.

"I'll give you a minute to look over the menu. Our specials are written on the board there." She pointed to a large chalkboard above the bar. "If you have any questions, Rose will be along shortly."

"Thank you." She smiled at the woman and started looking over the menu.

Rose was a beautiful looking woman who had a waist the size of Shelly's thigh. The woman's hair reached down all the way to her calves and was intricately weaved in long thin braids. Just hearing her accent made Shelly imagine warm summer nights and spicy foods.

"Where are you visiting from?" Rose asked with a hint of a Jamaican accent, sitting down across from Shelly, looking quite comfortable.

"I just moved here from DC." Shelly smiled. "Actually, I'm sort of your neighbor."

"Oh, really now?" Rose smiled. "Which place did you buy?"

"The old furniture shop a few doors down." She chuckled when Rose made a funny face. "It's not that bad, I swear."

"I don't know about dat." She frowned and shook her head. "Place ought to be burned and rebuilt. If'n you ask me."

Shelly laughed. "Well, I am in the market for a good contractor." She leaned forward. "If you know of any."

Rose frowned a little and tilted her head. "I know of someone who can help out. Give me a moment." She nodded. "I'll put your order in first, though." She smiled when Shelly's stomach chose that moment to let out a loud rumble.

Shelly laughed. "Thank you. My stomach and I appreciate it."

Just after her food was delivered, a dark-haired woman walked up to her table. Her long hair was tied back neatly away from her face. She had the most mesmerizing silver eyes Shelly had ever seen. She was smiling at her as she stood by her table.

"I hear you're in the market for a contractor."

Shelly nodded and set down the rest of her burger. "I just bought the old furniture shop a few doors down."

"I'm sorry." The woman chuckled and held out her hand. "I'm Cassey Grayton. I own Boardwalk Bar and Grill."

Shelly instantly felt jealous of the woman's sleek

clothing and sexy shoes and wished she'd had taken a little time to unpack some of her better clothes.

"Oh." Shelly reached up and shook her hand. "I'm Shelly Harrison. Soon to be owner of Shelly's Boutique." She motioned for Cassey to sit across from her.

"How wonderful." Cassey smiled and sat down. Shelly could see the woman assessing her. "I was wondering who had purchased the old place. A boutique?"

Shelly nodded. "I have some work to do first." She frowned as she took another sip of her drink.

"From the look of the outside, I'd say there's *a lot* of work that needs to be done." Cassey smiled.

"Yeah." Shelly nodded. "I guess the pictures my agent sent me didn't do it justice."

Cassey frowned. "If I remember correctly, there's an apartment above the place. You aren't staying there now, are you?" Shelly nodded. "So, have you talked to any contractor yet?" Cassey leaned forward a little.

Shelly shook her head and took a sip of her drink. "No, I just got into town this morning. I'm in the market for someone who's licensed and can work fast and cheap."

Cassey smile grew. "Wonderful, I have just the brother for you."

Marcus's whole body hurt. He threw his booted feet up on the solid oak desk in his office and closed his eyes. Damn if his brother wasn't working him to death.

Well, it wasn't really Roman's fault. After all, Marcus is the one who had accepted three jobs at once. But now that two of them were in the final stages, he was looking forward to finally getting some rest. Maybe he'd go with Cole on one of his surfing trips. His brother had recovered from the motorcycle accident he'd had last year and had doubled his efforts to get himself drowned in some of the largest waves around the world.

He chuckled to himself. Cole had enough trophies now that even he couldn't build big enough shelves to house them all. But he had to admit, even the thought of a warm beach and half-naked women didn't appeal to him all that much right now. No, what he wanted was a project with heart. Not one of these cookie-cutter ones he'd been working on lately.

Roman and he had started Paradise Construction a little over four years ago, just before Roman had opened Spring Haven Home for Boys. Roman ran both businesses, but everyone knew his heart was really in the home for kids. He doted on those kids and every time someone moved to a permanent home, his brother acted like he was walking on air.

Shaking his head, he thought that maybe it was time to start a special project for himself. After all, he was pushing twenty-five. Maybe he'd take a hint from his sister and settle down. He smiled thinking of Cassey and Luke, and how they'd ended up together.

Leaning his head back against the leather chair, he crossed his arms over his chest and moaned slightly at the muscles that screamed back at him.

He didn't normally do a lot of the heavy lifting on jobs, but this morning the foreman he'd hired for the South Baptist Church job had called him and told him he was short on drywall installers for the day. So he'd woken his butt up at five and had hauled enough Sheetrock up two flights of stairs to make his back sore. Who was he kidding? Everything on him was sore.

He had to admit it, though—he loved every minute of his job, from creating the plans for a new building to seeing the finished product. Every ounce of his creativity went into each nail and screw. He was born for taking something broken, something no one else wanted to touch, and turning it into something people oohed and head over.

Of course, it helped that he was making a good living from it. But what good was a bank load of money if he didn't enjoy it once in a while?

He shifted a little in the leather chair and was thankful Cassey had talked him into buying the executive chair for his new office. It was a hell of a lot more comfortable than sitting on the wooden folding chair he'd used before.

It wasn't that he was opposed to spending cash; it was more like he didn't have time to. Since helping Cassey rebuild the bar and grill last year, he'd been taking on job after job, including her fiancé's new hotel, which was due to open its doors in a few short weeks. Of course, he'd only overseen that job and had put his best men on it. He'd had to contract out most of the work since his heart was in remodeling projects, not starting from scratch.

Maybe it *was* time he took a few days off? His business wouldn't suffer if he did. He had a good bunch of guys working for him. Some of them had been there since the day he had started his business. Besides, Roman owed him one. He was positive he could talk his brother into watching over everything, at least for a short while.

He smiled a little to himself knowing just how to persuade his brother—blackmail.

He rested back as his mind conjured up images of lying

on a warm beach in Australia. Or maybe he'd head down to Mexico and go scuba diving. Images of tan women in barely any clothes popped into his head and he knew without a doubt it was time to take a break.

It had been months since he'd gone out on a date. Actually, maybe it had been a little longer than a few. He thought about it as he heard his phone beep with a new message.

He tried to ignore the annoying sound. Finally, what seemed like minutes later, it stopped, and he knew whatever Cassey wanted could wait. Oh, he knew it was her. She was the only one still up at this hour. He opened his right eye and tried to focus on the clock, but when it was too blurry to read the time, he closed it again.

He should have gone home, but he knew Roman had a date tonight. Sharing an apartment with his brother was becoming more of a pain in the butt than he could ever remember.

They each had their own rooms but try explaining how you live with your brother to a date. He shifted again and tried to get comfortable. Damn, why hadn't he bought that leather sofa for his office when Cassey had tried to talk him into it?

First thing in the morning, he was going sofa shopping. No, better yet, first thing in the morning he was going house shopping. Something old and along the beach. Something that needed a lot of work. If he was going to live in it, he was going to make it his first.

His mind raced over the small town of Surf Breeze. It was small enough that he knew almost every square inch of the place. There were several properties he could look into. Maybe the blue home on Crystal drive? Or the old three-story yellow house just down the road on Beach Front.

He was so busy mentally driving through the town looking for a house, that he hadn't heard his door open. When someone cleared their throat in front of him, he almost jumped out of his chair.

CHAPTER 3

Shelly stood over the sleeping man and felt her knees shake. He looked nothing like his sister. They both had dark hair, but that was as far as the resemblance went.

Marcus Grayton was sexy. Too sexy. She tried not to focus on how his long legs looked in his worn jeans, crossed up on the desk. Or how his wide chest looked full of all the right kind of muscles as his shirt stretched tightly over him.

His chin was covered with a full day of growth, giving him an even sexier look. Since his eyes were closed, she couldn't tell if he had silver eyes that matched his sister's. She thought that if he did, he'd be even more dangerously good-looking than he was with his eyes closed.

When Cassey had told her that her brother owned a construction company, she'd jumped at the contact. She'd asked for his number, but Cassey had smiled and tried to call and text him first. Then she'd called her other brother, Roman, who had informed her that Marcus was most likely at their office. She was happy to find out that was just a few doors down from her place.

"I'm sure he's still there," Cassey had said. "I'll text him that you're going to stop by on the way back to your place."

At first, she'd tried to convince her that she'd deal with it tomorrow, but Cassey had assured her that it was better to get him now, outside of normal business hours.

She had found his office easily enough. It was above the ice cream parlor like Cassey had said. There was a small sign, Paradise Construction, lit up in light blue hanging next to the office door.

When she reached for the door, she was amazed that it wasn't locked. When she'd walked in and noticed that he was asleep behind his desk, she'd thought about turning around and walking out again. But then she'd gotten a look at him and something had held her in place.

Realizing she'd been standing there looking at him for well over a minute, she cleared her throat. If he didn't wake, she'd quietly turn around and leave, then return first thing in the morning. His eyes flew open and zeroed in on her as his body jumped slightly.

"I'm sorry." She cleared her throat again, trying not to smile.

He blinked a few times and slowly unfolded his arms from across his chest. Then shook his head.

"Cassey called you." She fiddled with her fingers and when his blue eyes dropped to watch the motion, she shoved them behind her back.

He shook his head again as his eyes focused on her. "I didn't answer."

"Yes, well, I know. She told me to stop by your office."

He dropped his legs from the top of the desk and nodded. "And here you are."

She smiled. "I'm Shelly Harrison. I purchased the place two doors down."

He frowned. "The old furniture store?"

She nodded. "I was just having dinner at your sister's place and she told me about you."

His eyes shot up and a slow smile crossed his lips. She noticed a sexy little dimple at the corner of his mouth and, for just a moment, her eyes couldn't focus on anything else.

When he didn't respond, she blinked a few times and tried to remember what she'd just said. Realizing the conversation could have taken any number of turns since she hadn't been listening, she fumbled for control.

"I'm in need of a contractor," she blurted out. "My place needs a lot of work."

He nodded as his smile grew a little more. "I figured it might."

"Yes, well," She cleared her throat again and tried like mad not to fidget with her hands. "I was…"

"You shouldn't be walking around without a jacket. Even though it's still warm during the day, the wind will give you the chills after the sun is down."

She blinked a few times. "I'm fine." She tried to start over, but he shook his head.

"You keep clearing your throat. Sounds like you've already caught something." He frowned and stood up. He moved towards her and she took a slight step back. "Here." He handed her a brown jacket that was tossed over the edge of a tall file cabinet. "Wear this as we walk."

"Walk?" She took the jacket from him absentmindedly.

"Sure." He smiled. "In order to work on your place, I'll have to see it first." He helped her on with the jacket, then walked to the door and held it open.

"Yes, well." She frowned as the warmth of the coat made her realize she'd been chilled before. "I hadn't planned on—"

He shook his head. "No time like the present." He waited. Something in his eyes told her that he would stand there all night if needed.

She walked over to him as she shoved her hands deep into his jacket pockets. He shut the door behind them softly and when she turned to say something, she bumped squarely into his chest. His hands came up to her shoulders and she took a giant step backward as his hands dropped to his sides.

"Sorry," he mumbled as he moved slowly around her and held the outer door open for her to walk through. She avoided his eyes as she moved past him and out onto the landing. She waited as he locked the door.

"What are you going to sell?" he asked as they walked down the wide steps that led up to the balcony. He reached the bottom and turned back and looked to where she was standing on the last step.

"Lots of things." She sighed and watched people walking along the boardwalk. Even after dark, there were still plenty of people strolling along, even in the chill of the winter night. She turned back to him when she realized he was standing there quietly watching, waiting for her. "I plan on opening a boutique store. Clothing, shoes, and purses. The kinds of things that tourists who flew to the area could enjoy and yet locals would still utilize."

He nodded then moved aside to let her step all the way down. "Do I hear a little Boston in your voice?"

The question threw her for a moment; she hadn't thought about being from Boston for a long time. She had grown up there, but her family had moved to Philadelphia when she was eleven, shortly after the family trip to Surf Breeze. Recently she had been living in DC. When she slowly nodded, he smiled.

"I haven't been up north in years." He sighed. "I hear they got dumped on a few weeks back. I can only remember seeing snow once in my life."

For a moment she thought that she saw the longing in those deep blue eyes of his. But when he blinked, the emotion was gone. He smiled slowly and started walking towards her new place.

"What made you decide on Surf Breeze?"

She shrugged her shoulders and easily matched his lazy pace. "My family vacationed here when I was young." She looked off towards the dark water and vaguely remembered the last good time she'd had with her parents before all the fighting and cheating had taken over their lives.

"Yeah, this place used to be something." He glanced at her. "Going to be again soon. It's starting to get there." He smiled. "Course, I've had a huge hand in turning these places around, myself."

She nodded. "That's what your sister said." She stopped in front of her place and nodded to him. "Well, what do you think?"

His eyes roamed over her tight body and his mind was flooded with pictures of what he'd like to do with her, to her. Shaking his head clear, he forced his eyes and mind to focus on the empty building that stood in front of them. It needed a lot of work before any inspector would allow customers to set foot in there.

The front windows would need to be replaced. Maybe even enlarged so product could be shown to passersby. The awning and the old sign above it would have to go; even standing here he wondered what was keeping them up.

Shaking his head, he stopped her from walking towards the front door. "Those need to go." He nodded above the door.

She stopped and looked up with a slight frown. When she nodded, her eyes slowly made their way down to their joined hands. He hadn't realized he'd kept hold of her or how much he enjoyed feeling her cool, small hand in his.

Dropping her hand, he shoved his deep into his pocket to fight off the chill in the air and to keep himself from touching her again. "Is there a back door?"

She nodded and started walking to the side of the building. He followed her and tried not to wonder if the rest of her would feel as good as her hand had.

When they stepped into the place and she flipped on several lights, flooding the main floor with bright light, his mind changed gears.

The room was silent as he walked around and took mental notes of what would need to be done. Old carpet would need to be ripped out. A wall could be taken down to give the appearance of a larger space. Paint. New lighting.

All in all, it was a good space. Nothing he hadn't transformed before. He'd have to officially sit down with her and go over her thoughts and plans for the space, but he had a few ideas swimming around in his mind.

The electrical and plumbing would have to be checked and updated. He knew that much from his experience working on the other buildings along the boardwalk.

There was a small staircase along the back wall that had been boarded off at the top, reminding him that she had living space upstairs that she'd mentioned needed some work.

When he was done assessing everything, Shelly was leaning against the back countertop, watching him.

"Don't you need to take notes?" She rested her chin in her hands and watched him.

"No." He shook his head and tapped his temple. "It's all locked up here."

"Well?" she said as she straightened and walked towards him. "What do you think?"

He smiled and moved closer to her. "I think there's a lot to do here before you can open your doors."

"I know that." She frowned a little. "But do you think you can handle it?"

He chuckled. "Lady, I can handle anything." He glanced around again. "We'll need to go over exactly what it is you want in here first, but I can work up an estimate and have it to you by tomorrow afternoon." He started walking towards the back door and then turned towards her again. "Use this door instead of the front one until I can have my men come tomorrow and take down the sign and awning out front. It's a hazard." He shook his head.

"Wait," she called after him and rushed towards him. "I'd like to see the estimate before I agree to…"

He stopped her and shook his head. "It's on me. Don't worry about it. They need to come down for the safety of people walking by." He turned back towards the door. "See you tomorrow," he called over his shoulder.

By the time he stepped out on the boardwalk again, he was wishing for his bed. Pulling his cell phone out of his pocket, he texted his brother and stood on the empty boardwalk, watching the dark waves hit the beach as he is waiting for a reply.

When he heard the door open and close behind him, he glanced over and watched Shelly lock the back door. She looked over at him and nodded, giving him a nervous smile, then she started up the stairs towards what he could only assume was the apartment.

"Didn't you say you need some work up there as well?" he asked, moving a little closer to her.

She stopped her hand on the railing and nodded at him. "I can show you around there tomorrow when it's light. Goodnight." She turned and started heading up the stairs and he watched her disappear. He knew that he'd dream that night about a sexy, hazel-eyed woman with pouty lips that just begged to be kissed.

CHAPTER 4

Shelly wasn't fully awake when she heard the crash. At first, she thought it was something lingering from her dream, but then she heard a string of curse words and her eyes flew open. Rushing to the window, she looked down and was shocked to see the old sign above her front door splattered all over the walkway below.

Glass and plastic pieces were strewn everywhere. There were also large metal chunks that looked very sharp and dangerous.

"What the hell! I told you to wait." She hunted for the voice and when her eyes landed on Marcus, she sighed at how handsome he looked in his work jeans and a button-up flannel shirt. "Damn near landed on top of me." He took off his hard hat and swiped a handkerchief over his forehead. Then, as if she'd willed it, he glanced up at the window and stilled.

She couldn't move. She couldn't even breathe. His blue eyes seemed to laugh until they caught hers. Then she swore she could feel the heat from them up here. He slowly smiled, causing heat to spread through her entire body. Her knees even felt a little weak. How could one look from him cause her body to react so?

She knew. It was because of the dreams she'd had last night. She'd fallen asleep thinking about how sexy he'd looked and how kind he'd been, and he'd stayed in her dreams all night.

Someone walked over to him and slapped him on the back while laughing, which caused his attention to drift from her.

She used that opportunity to dash from the window and head towards the bathroom to get ready for the day. When she walked into the restroom, she glanced at her reflection and gasped. She'd forgotten that she'd fallen asleep in a white tank top and her silk undies. Glancing back towards the window, she realized that the windowsill was low enough to give Marcus quite a view.

Her face turned red and she closed her eyes on a moan.

"Great! Give everyone a show, why don't you?" She flipped on the shower. The old pipes groaned, and she held her breath as cold water poured from the showerhead.

The upstairs of the building had originally been part of the furniture store. Somewhere along the way, the stairs had been demolished and moved to the outside of the building, only allowing entrance from outside.

The upstairs was as large as the lower level and housed a small bathroom and kitchenette area. Her air mattress sat along the wall with a stack of her boxes.

She felt lucky that the upstairs bathroom was equipped with a small shower. She had high hopes of adding a bathtub but knew that if it wasn't in her budget, she'd have to make do. After all, the downstairs was more important than her own living space.

After one of the quickest and coldest showers she'd had in a long time, she piled her hair up in a clip and donned an older pair of jeans and a work shirt. Slipping on her old tennis shoes, she grabbed the sketches she'd drawn up last night and headed outside to see the progress.

When she reached the bottom of the outside stairs, she wrapped her arms around herself and watched as Marcus and three other men used a small lift to take down the awning that hung over the whole storefront.

It took all their concentration to work it down to the sidewalk in front of the doors.

When it finally rested on solid ground, she stepped forward.

"It looks very heavy," she said coming up behind Marcus. He turned and nodded.

"The thing is old. They use a new, lighter material now, but they used to be made from steel." He nodded to where the sign and awning used to be on the building. "If you want an awning, I can give you information on a good company in town that will give you a great price. But for now, at least you won't have to worry about it coming down on anyone's head."

She smiled. The building looked better without them. She planned on having a sign above the door, but something smaller and more elegant. As for the awning, she was glad the ugly thing was down. The torn brown and green material was the only thing she hadn't liked about the front of her building.

Turning back to Marcus, she held out the folder she'd

carried downstairs with her. "I have a few things I'd like to go over with you if you have the time."

He nodded. "Let me just have these guys haul this all away." He nodded to the mess, then turned back to her and frowned. "You forgot a jacket again. Head inside. I'll be just a moment."

She nodded and pulled out her keys and stepped carefully around the mess. Unlocking the front doors, she walked inside and headed straight back to what would become her cashiers' area. Currently, there was a large display case that she had plans to renovate and utilize for some of her smaller items.

She knew exactly what she wanted to have in her store and she looked around the space and imagined just how it would be. She'd always had an eye for design. She loved looking at a space and planning what would make it look more inviting, more personal, or more professional.

She'd wanted to go to school for design, but her parents had had other plans. She frowned, thinking of her parents, as she looked down at the growing list on her tablet.

This was the only thing she'd ever done without their approval or without them even knowing. She'd told them her plans several years ago, but they had laughed and assumed she was joking. She hadn't *encouraged* them to believe that she'd take her inheritance from Nanna and move south to follow her dreams. Her parents still believed she was living in the large townhouse they'd bought her near the school and that she was finishing off the last two years they demanded from her. After all, no Harrison would ever be caught dead without at least a Ph.D. She sighed and closed her eyes and tried not to think of how much she was going to disappoint her family.

"Problem?" His voice instantly stole her attention from her family issues. Since her eyes were closed, she could hear just how sexy he sounded. When she opened them, she tried not to let her thoughts show on her face, but she could tell that he'd guessed because his smile was quick and potent.

Shaking her head, no, she coughed and focused on what she'd wanted to talk to him about.

He walked over to her and placed his jacket over her shoulders. "I told you it's pretty cold outside and in here." He walked over to the thermostat on the back wall. Shaking his head, he cranked it up a few notches and then turned to her as he rubbed his hands together. "This may be a lot warmer than where you're used to, but it's still cold enough to make you sick."

She shook her head. "I'm not sick." How could she tell him that the cough was a nervous twitch he caused in her?

"Right." He nodded. His smile and eyes told her that he didn't believe her.

Still, she pushed her chilled arms through the long sleeves of his jacket until the room warmed up a little.

"What's all this?" he asked and nodded to the drawings she'd set out. He walked over and started looking through her sketches.

"Some ideas I had." She stepped next to him and watched him flip through her sketches. His eyes scanned every detail. Then they ran over her notes and the supply lists she had printed out.

When he was done, he turned towards her and leaned

on the cabinet. "We could make this work." He tapped her sketches.

"Which parts?" She itched to go over every detail with him, step by step.

"All of it." He chuckled. "There's nothing in here that isn't doable. I suppose it will all depend on what you had set aside for your remodel budget."

She grabbed up her tablet and opened the spreadsheet that showed the amounts.

She handed it to him, but he backed away a little, putting his hands behind his back.

She chuckled. "It's just a tablet. I have my budget—"

He shook his head again when she tried to hand it to him. "I... I'm not good with those things. It surprises me that my cell phone is still ticking."

She would have laughed at him, but the sincerity in his eyes stopped her.

She sighed and glanced down at the numbers and spouted them off quickly—how much she had set aside for construction, for the sign that would hang above the door, how much she estimated new flooring would cost. She'd done her homework and she'd been very thorough.

When she was done, he chuckled. "Want a job?"

She looked up at him and hugged the tablet to her chest. "I'm sorry?"

He shook his head. "That has to be one of the most accurate and detailed lists I've ever heard."

She smiled a little. "Thank you."

"There shouldn't be a problem with those figures if you could..." He looked down at the tablet in question.

"I can email these to you?"

He nodded his head. "Send them to my brother's

email." He handed her a card. "He's the financial genius in our family."

"Your sister told me there were two of you. Does he just work behind the scenes?"

He nodded his head. "Most of the time, but sometimes I let him out and shove a hammer in his hand." He smiled, and she couldn't stop herself from smiling with him.

"I always wished I had a brother or sister around."

He leaned a little more on the cabinet. "Only child, huh?"

She nodded. "Are there just the three of you?"

He shook his head no. "Another brother." He chuckled. "If he's still alive today. And a sister we haven't seen in a while." She blinked and looked at him in question. "My brother is Cole Grayton." He waited and when she shook her head, he laughed. "Oh, this is rich. Wait until he meets you." He chuckled some more. "Cole's head could use a little deflating."

"Is he a movie star or something?"

"Not yet. He's a surfer. Been on too many billboards to count, flaunting everything God gave him in just his boxers." He shook his head and a little of the smile died away. "'Bout killed himself riding some crazy storm waves. Almost finished the job last year in a motorcycle accident."

She vaguely remembered hearing something about a surfer who had been in a bad motorcycle accident but couldn't remember the details.

"He's back in Sydney this month." He shook his head. "The accident didn't even slow him down." He sighed.

"What about your sister?" She leaned a little on the

cabinet and watched his eyes turn soft. He looked a little lost. "The other one."

"Took off on us a few days after her seventeenth birthday." He closed his eyes and she could see that he was fighting back some emotion. He shook his head and when he opened his eyes, he'd changed back to humor. "Now it's your turn."

"What?" She stood up again, putting a little more space between them.

"Share and tell. I shared a little, now you get to tell me something." He smiled and leaned on the countertop

Her smile fell away and she felt her heart skip a little. She didn't like talking about her family. To be honest with herself, she didn't like even thinking about her family.

"So, your family is from Boston?" The question hung in the air.

Marcus watched her whole demeanor change. She went from relaxed and friendly to ice princess in under two seconds flat. Her entire body went rigid.

Reaching out, he gripped her arm before she could walk away. "Hey?" he said softly. "Didn't mean to spook you." He would do anything to see the smile and laughter he'd witnessed a few minutes ago return.

She shook her head and started gathering up her sketches. Sketches, he had to admit, that equaled the ones that he'd drawn up of her place. She had talent and, he'd bet his teeth, education.

What he couldn't put his finger on was why she was here, trying to open a nickel-and-dime store. But after seeing her reaction to the mention of her family, he'd wager it had everything to do with them.

"You didn't. I don't like talking about them, that's all." She sighed and closed the folder with her sketches tucked away. "You can take these if you need."

He took them from her, knowing she'd effectively ended the conversation. There were a few ideas she'd drawn up that he hadn't thought of. It was always a good idea to follow what the client wanted, anyway. Besides, they would help Roman with the estimate, which he'd planned on getting to her later that evening.

"If it's okay, I'd like to take a look upstairs now."

She nodded and walked slowly towards the door. He followed her and saw her back relax a little as she walked. Then at the top of the outer stairs, she turned to him.

"I'm sorry." She sighed. "It's just that I'm not very close with my family."

"Hey, no need to apologize." He smiled. "I know the feeling."

Her eyebrows shot up and then a little line formed between them. "But, you just got done telling me…"

He chuckled and interrupted her. "I don't talk about my real family." He shook his head. "We were all adopted by the Graytons." He smiled. "Great people. But my real folks…" He shook his head and stiffened when memories of his mother's face popped into his mind, just like Shelly had a few minutes ago. "They're a different story," he said in a low voice.

He watched understanding cross her eyes. "I wondered when I didn't see the resemblance between you and Cassey." She smiled. "You would have never guessed it by the way she went on talking about you." She stopped with her hand on the doorknob. "Do you know, I actually thought at one point she was thinking about setting us up?"

He laughed. "I wouldn't be surprised. Since she and Luke started living a happily blissful life, she's been trying to set me up more and more." He had luckily escaped the first two attempts, but he was starting to wonder if his sister hadn't succeeded in her third attempt.

She smiled and pushed open the door to what would be her apartment. Downstairs, his creative mind had been focused on business, but up here, his design imagination started going wild.

They walked into a large room with high ceilings and exposed ventilation. The whole left side of the building was exposed brick that, with a little work, could be refurbished. The hardwood floors would have to be sanded and stained and might need a few coats of lacquer to make them shine.

There was a very small kitchen area off to the other side with what he assumed was a small bathroom behind it. Everything else was open and exposed, one big great room for him to do whatever he wanted with.

He walked around the room in silence as he planned everything out. He frowned when he noticed the air mattress sitting against a wall by a dozen unpacked boxes. She should be in a hotel, he thought, not sleeping on the floor. Better yet, she should be in a large poster bed with a canopy of silk covering her.

Shaking his head, he turned back to the room and imagined a large king-sized bed made of dark wood sitting in the corner behind a half wall that separated the space from the rest of the room, a soft white canopy of silk draping down from each poster.

He laughed inwardly. This wasn't where his experience was. He was a builder. He remodeled things, not designed them.

Walking into the small bathroom, he shook his head and thought of a plan to expand it, adding a closet for her clothes and storage. She would want a tub; every woman wanted a tub. Maybe something with jets. He turned and looked at her back as she watched people below. Yeah, definitely jets. He smiled and made a mental note to check on a few different options.

The old shower would have to go. Most of the tiles were just barely hanging on. When he turned on the faucet, the old pipes kicked, and he knew there was some updating needed there. It took too long for the hot water to hit, and even then, it was lukewarm, so he added a new tankless water heater to his mental list. The toilet and sink were so outdated, he immediately added those, as well.

He walked back out to the main room. The lighting would need to be updated, and he'd have to add electric for new appliances in the kitchen. He looked around and thought that he'd move the whole kitchen to the other side, in front of the stairs so that the brick wall was completely bare. That side he would save for her living space and a small dining area.

"Well?" she asked as he walked up beside her. The windows were tall, starting around their knees and going all the way up. Some of the windows would have to be replaced. It would be best if all of them could be replaced with double-paned windows, but he doubted she had a budget to cover the cost.

"You've got a nice space here." He looked out at her view. The boardwalk was below them and he watched for a moment as people strolled by. Beyond that was a long strip of beach and then the emerald water. It was a calm day and barely any waves rippled the water, which made it look green for as far as the eye could see.

He turned towards her and noticed that some soft strands of her blonde hair had fallen around her face. She had either forgotten to put on makeup that morning or had very little on. Her skin looked so soft, he itched to reach out and touch it. His eyes roamed over her and he couldn't deny the sudden and powerful tug he got from looking at her curves. She was taller than most women he'd dated. He gauged her height around five-eight. The old jeans she was wearing were snug in all the right places, making him wish he could run his hands over those long legs.

When she turned her eyes towards him, catching him in his assessment of her, he couldn't stop the smile.

"Beautiful view," he said, softly.

CHAPTER 5

"Yes," she said under her breath, holding in a sigh. Her knees threatened to give out on her, and she was finding it very hard to concentrate on breathing. She heard a light buzzing in her head and took a few deep breaths before she embarrassed herself further by fainting under his heated gaze. "I had hoped that some of these windows would open." She turned her eyes back to the view and tried hard not to feel the heat radiating from the man standing next to her. Frowning a little, she looked at the large wall of glass and wished to hear the ocean.

"That could be arranged. Did you have some sketches for up here?"

She turned back to him and shook her head. "I haven't had time yet. I could—"

He shook his head, stopping her. "Why don't you just tell me what you had in mind, instead."

She smiled and explained how she'd dreamed of turning the open space into her new home.

An hour later, she watched from the large windows as he walked back towards his small office a few doors down. She saw him stop and talk to a few people. He looked and acted like he belonged here. Like he'd always been here. She sighed and longed for that feeling. It had been years since she'd really felt like she fit in. Even at college, she'd always felt like an outsider. Maybe it was because she'd been living in a large townhouse in the wealthiest part of town instead of in the dorms with the rest of the kids.

Crossing her arms over her chest, she watched people enjoying the small waves and the sugar soft sand.

The first thing she'd done yesterday after walking through her building was to walk down to the water's edge with her shoes off and feel the cold water and soft sand. She'd forgotten how soft it was. Sighing, she turned back towards her room and started unpacking her boxes. Since she didn't have a closet yet, she folded all of her clothes and put them on the long shelf that ran along the back wall, using the small area as a makeshift changing room since it was sheltered from the large windows along the front of the building.

After spending a little over an hour sweeping and cleaning the upstairs, she decided a long walk on the beach was just what she needed.

At some point, she would have to hit a grocery store for some basic items, but until she felt a little more centered, she wanted to enjoy these little moments and— for the first time in her life—her freedom.

She was thankful Marcus hadn't continued to ask her about her past. Once she'd made it clear to him that she didn't want to talk about her family, he'd changed the subject.

Just knowing that he had been adopted made her wonder more about him and Cassey and their other siblings.

He'd mentioned that he didn't talk about his real parents, but it didn't stop her from wondering about them. Much like, she was sure, he was wondering about hers.

She changed into an old pair of flip-flops and left them along with many others next to the steps that led down to the beach. The long hike across the white sand to get to the water's edge was exhilarating. It was strange, but from above, it hadn't looked that far to the water. By the time she'd reached the cool water, she was almost out of breath.

She used to be in excellent shape, back when her mother had enrolled her in several dance classes. But when she'd started high school, her mother had replaced them with early college classes instead.

Vowing to start jogging every day, she walked briskly along the shoreline, only stopping a handful of times to pick up shells.

By the time she made it back to the boardwalk, she had a pocket full of sand dollars the size of nickels and quarters. Her other pocket had two medium-sized conch shells, one of them completely white.

Slipping on her shoes again, she decided to find someplace for lunch. Her stomach hadn't stopped complaining for the last half an hour. She'd seen the little bakery called the Lunch Box and decided a sandwich was in order.

When she walked in, she was greeted by a friendly looking silver-haired man dressed in shorts and a brightly colored shirt.

"Hello, sweetie. What can I get you to drink today?"

She looked up at the carefully written menu on the

chalkboard behind him. "Raspberry iced tea sounds wonderful." She smiled.

"Oh, a native." He smiled at her and for a moment, she thought he'd realized she owned the building a dozen doors down. "Boston, right?"

She smiled. "I guess I just can't hide it around here." When his eyebrows shot up in question, she continued. "That's the second time I've been asked that in two days."

"Oh?" He smiled. "It took me living down here fifteen years before people stopped asking me." He smiled. "I'll grab that tea for you." He turned to go but looked over his shoulder. "The specials today are right there." He pointed to the side of the chalkboard. "Take your time deciding."

She was so engrossed in the menu; she didn't realize someone had sat next to her until they spoke.

"I saw you talking with Cassey last night, correct?"

When Shelly turned, she was surprised at how beautiful the blonde woman sitting next to her was. Her long hair was tied back in a fancy braid, exposing the most beautiful face and skin Shelly had ever seen. The woman's smile was perfect. Every tooth was as white as freshly fallen snow. Shelly's eyes took in everything about her. Her clothes were light and stylish. Shelly felt small and plain sitting next to the woman. It was all quite intimidating. All she could do was nod her head.

"I'm Wendy. I bartend at Boardwalk Bar and Grill." She held out her hand, waiting for Shelly to take it.

"Shelly." She took her hand and shook it. "I just purchased the furniture store a few doors down."

"That's what I thought. Cassey couldn't stop talking about you last night. I've been too busy to come over, but I'm glad I bumped into you today." When the woman smiled, her eyes lit up. Could this woman be interested in her? Her face started to heat with embarrassment. Shelly waited, feeling a little awkward and not sure what to say. What could this woman possibly want from her? She hadn't really had any friends growing up, except the kids that her parents forced her to hang around. And she'd never been hit on by a woman before.

Wendy chuckled a little. "I'm not coming on to you." She leaned a little closer and bumped her shoulder with hers. "Although, you are pretty sexy in those work clothes." She giggled at her joke.

Shelly looked down and realized she was still wearing her dusty pants and shirt from before. She really had to start thinking about how she dressed when she went out.

Just then, the older man delivered her tea. "How's it going, Wendy? I'll be with you in a shake." He smiled and then turned back to Shelly. "Have you decided yet?"

"Yes, I'll have the special. Can I get a side of potato soup with that?"

He nodded and then turned to Wendy. "Your usual?"

Wendy laughed. "It is Wednesday." She leaned on the counter and placed her chin in her hands as the man walked away to put in their orders.

"That's Marvin. He and Alfred own this place." She turned around on the bar stool and leaned back on the counter, so she could watch people outside. "Cassey said you were going to open a boutique of sorts?"

Shelly nodded and took a large sip of her tea. The sweetness hit her as the liquid cooled her off. She hadn't realized how warm it was outside.

"Yes, I'm hoping to open by spring break."

"Wow," she said, kicking her feet a little. "The place

sure does need a lot of work. Have you met with hunk number one yet?"

"I'm sorry?" She twisted a little to watch people walk by outside like Wendy was doing.

"You know Cassey's big fun brother, Marcus. Hunk number one out of three." She smiled and glanced at her.

"Oh." Shelly nodded. "Yes, last night and again this morning."

Wendy whistled and shook her head. "Twice in so many hours. Be careful, he might grow on you." She winked. "The Grayton boys have a way of either pissing you off or making you completely fall for them." Wendy's eyes saddened, and she turned around quickly.

Was this woman trying to tell Shelly something? Did she have a thing for Marcus? All of a sudden, Shelly realized she hardly knew anything about him, yet she'd already decided that their relationship had the potential to go somewhere.

Now, everything was clearer. That's why Wendy had hunted her down. To stake her territory. Well, Shelly wasn't one to trample on anyone's toes.

"I only met with him because I needed the work done. I didn't realize..." She dropped off as Wendy spun back towards her, a look of confusion on her face.

"Didn't realize what?" she asked as she reached over and took a drink from the water that Marvin had just delivered.

She looked down at her tea, then back at the woman. "That you two were an item."

Wendy laughed. Not just a little chuckle, but a loud, whole-body laugh. After about a minute of listening to her, Shelly couldn't stop herself from smiling along with her.

"Oh, that's rich. Wait until I tell him that joke." She pretended to wipe a tear from her eye. "No, Marcus and I are just buds."

Then it dawned on her. She'd been talking about one of his brothers. Her mouth dropped open and she let her lips make an "O."

"Yeah, not there either." She shook her head. "Although I would like to kill one of them." She winked at her again. "I'll let you figure out which one though."

Shelly laughed. "I haven't met any of the others yet."

"Oh, you will. They never stray too far."

Just then, their food arrived, and Shelly laughed when she saw that Wendy had gotten the special as well. The roasted turkey panini looked fabulous. She bit into it and realized it was better than sandwiches she'd paid top dollar for.

"Now you know why I come here for lunch every Wednesday." Wendy smiled at her as she took another bite of her own sandwich.

She enjoyed her conversation with Wendy over lunch. The woman was a talker. She'd asked Shelly a few questions, but when it was clear that she didn't like talking about herself, Wendy had started talking about anyone and everyone she knew. Shelly thought she was trying to familiarize her with the locals a little. By the time her sandwich and soup were gone, she felt like she knew more about the small town of Surf Breeze than she knew about the town where she'd grown up.

"Of course, Blanco Beach is the best beach," Wendy said, leaning closer to her whispering, "But don't tell anyone else." She sighed. "The beaches have quite the competition going between themselves."

Wendy had told her that the locals didn't really say they were from a specific town, but rather which beach they lived closest to. Blanco Beach was the beach just outside her front door. The name was fitting.

"Of course, this whole stretch of the Gulf has white sand, but we have the best sandbar. Just wait, this summer when you can hit the warm water, you'll see." She smiled as they walked out of the little cafe together. Wendy stopped and nodded to the water. "Right there. You can wade out about a hundred feet and plop down on your butt and enjoy. Course, some people complain that the surf isn't strong enough, or that you can't ride the waves." She frowned a little and looked off to the water.

Shelly saw concern in her eyes. Wendy shook her head and turned back to her with a smile.

"Now, if you need any help with your place, let me or Cassey know." She smiled. "Oh, you should stop by the bar and grill Friday night. We have a live band coming in. The Wailers. They're one of my favorites."

Shelly walked back up her stairs feeling like she'd just made her very first real friend.

Marcus walked into his bathroom and sighed. All he wanted was a hot shower and a few hours to plop down in front of the TV and shut his mind off, but he knew there was a stack of papers his brother had worked up for Shelly which needed to be hand delivered.

"Sure you don't want me to swing by and deliver those?" Roman had asked when he'd handed them to him.

His brother had a different kind of look about him.

Where Cole had a surfer, beach bum look, and Marcus was rough and rugged, Roman was clean-cut and professional looking. Women ate his kind up. He could hardly remember a time when Roman didn't have someone mooning after him. He and Cole couldn't complain in that department, either, but Roman had a way with women they would never have.

Marcus didn't want him anywhere near Shelly yet, so he'd told him that he had a few more design questions he had to go over with her. Roman had seen straight through his lie, but his dark eyes had softened, and he'd said he was going to swing by Spring Haven Home that evening.

Spring Haven Home was an idea Marcus had talked to Roman about years ago when they were still scraping their knees climbing trees and trying to build the best tree house. He'd actually forgotten about the idea until Roman had driven him by an old house in Spring Haven and shown him the business plan.

It had taken a little over a year for the two of them to remodel the old place into something that could be used as a group foster home.

They'd started Paradise Construction to help pay for the place, and after Cassey opened her bar and grill, she'd started pitching some extra money in as well. It took a few yearly fundraisers and a whole lot of work on Roman's part to keep the home up and running, but it was his baby. Marcus hadn't expected it, since out of all the kids, Marcus was the only one who'd spent time at a place like it.

He supposed it was because Roman loved kids. His brother couldn't get enough of them, actually. He spent most of his free time down at the place working with the kids. He planned outings, crafts—you name it, Roman was there. Not only did his brother have the best business mind in the clan, he was Peter freaking Pan while he was at it.

After grabbing a quick shower to rinse off the sweat and grime he'd earned helping his men finish off the McCallister's renovated attic, he pulled on a pair of his nicer khakis and a button-up shirt. Might as well take a hint from his brother and look the part. Glancing at himself in the mirror, he smiled. He didn't like dressing up. Hell, he was most comfortable in shorts, a T-shirt, and flip-flops. That or old jeans, dusty shirts, and work boots.

He pulled the comb through his wet hair and put on a dash of aftershave. Not that he was trying to impress her. Hell, okay, he couldn't lie to himself. He *was* trying to impress her. Why not? He was young and unattached, and Shelly was beautiful, and as far as he could tell, unattached as well.

Tucking the large folder his brother had given him under his arm, he grabbed his keys and jogged out the door. It was only a few blocks to the boardwalk and the evening air was warm enough, so he decided to walk instead of hunting for a parking spot.

When he got to the top of her stairs, he could tell that she wasn't there, and all of the nerves and excitement that had built up from the thought of seeing her dissipated. He stood at the top of the steps in the now fading light and wondered what to do. Maybe he'd head over to Cassey's place for a while and check back later? Just as he turned to go, he saw her start to climb the stairs, hidden behind three large grocery bags. She was talking to herself and he leaned back and enjoyed the show.

When she was halfway up the stairs, she spotted him

and almost dropped the third bag, which was balanced between the other two.

"Oh!" She closed her eyes for a second and he could hear her breathing speed up.

"Sorry." He chuckled. "Didn't mean to scare you." He raced down the stairs and took two of her bags before she dropped them.

"Thanks," she said a little breathlessly as she reached out and took a hold of the railing to steady herself.

He noticed that she'd changed into a long cream-colored skirt with a rose-colored blouse. She'd piled her hair up while letting those soft strands fall around her face.

"I absolutely fell in love with the little grocery store two blocks away," she said quickly. "I probably bought too much, though." She frowned, looking at the three bags.

He chuckled. "I always do. That's why Roman took over the shopping a year back."

"Oh?" She turned slightly and looked at him as she unlocked her door.

"My brother and I moved in together right after school." He shrugged his shoulders as he walked in behind her. "Guess we never saw any reason not to live together." Until recently, he wanted to add but didn't.

"That's nice. It must be wonderful to have someone who's always there for you." She set her bag down on the small countertop.

He could hear the loneliness in her voice. When he set the two bags down, he glanced at her.

"Are you sure you have enough room for all of this?" He stood back as she started pulling items out of the bags.

She laughed and shook her head. "No, not really. It's a good thing I didn't go overboard with cold items." She leaned down to place a few items into the small refrigerator. "Have you eaten?" she asked, glancing over her shoulder.

He shook his head. "I was planning on swinging by Cassey's place after I dropped these off to you." He held up the folder.

"Oh?" She continued to put away her items.

"Roman finished the bid for you. I have a few design ideas in here as well." He stood back and watched her quickly empty the bags.

"Why don't you stay? We can go over everything after dinner. I was going to make some Chicken Alfredo." She had her back to him so she couldn't see the quick air pump he did behind her back.

"Sounds good." He leaned against the counter. "Can I help?"

She glanced at him. "There's a bottle of wine in here somewhere." She looked into the last bag. "Here." She handed it to him, then searched in a drawer for a corkscrew. "You can pour." She smiled at him. "Glasses are there." She pointed to her one and only cupboard next to the fridge.

Taking down two wine glasses, he shook his head as he opened the bottle. "Still don't know where you plan on putting all that."

She frowned at him. "I'm trying to figure that out myself." She leaned back and sighed. "I suppose it's going to be a while before everything starts feeling like a home around here."

He nodded. "We could start up here first."

She shook her head no. "I don't mind roughing it for a

while. I'd rather get started downstairs." She turned and pulled out a large pan. "I met Wendy today."

"Oh?" He chuckled. "And you still have both your ears I see."

She smiled. "It was very nice of her to fill me in on all that goes on around here."

"I'm sure she did." He handed her a glass of wine."

She stopped and took a sip. "For a moment, I thought she was trying to ward me off."

"From?" He leaned against the counter and watched as she moved around the small kitchen. She looked like she knew what she was doing, so he guessed he wouldn't have to fake liking her dinner.

"You," she said as she glanced over her shoulder.

He'd just taken a sip of his wine, and he started choking it back up. She rushed over to him and started pounding on his back to help him.

CHAPTER 6

She didn't know what had made her say that, but his response made her start questioning his relationship with the busty blonde all over again.

"My God!" he said when he could finally breathe again. "That's just rich." When he started laughing, she could only sit back and watch. "And they call me the funny one." He shook his head and quickly downed another large sip of wine.

"Sorry?" She turned and started working on dinner again. She hadn't meant to pry, but it had been eating at her all day. If Wendy didn't feel that way about Marcus, she wondered if Marcus felt that way about someone else. After all, she didn't really know anything about him yet.

"No." He shook his head. "Wendy and I are just friends. Actually, I kind of think of her as a sister. Not that I've known her that long, two or three years now, but..." He shrugged his shoulders. "We're just very close friends." He leaned closer to her and gave her a lopsidedness smile. "Now, I can't say the same for my brother." He chuckled.

"I'm curious to know which one. She mentioned she wished one of the Grayton men would take a... how did she put it? Long walk off a short pier?"

He laughed. "Yes, she and Cole just rub each other wrong. When he got into his motorcycle accident last year, she actually chewed him out in front of my father and aunt at the hospital." He laughed. "Cole was hooked up to all these machines and covered in bandages, and she stood over him berating him about trying to kill himself."

She frowned as she diced up the chicken and tossed it in the hot pan. "That couldn't have been good for your family."

He shook his head with a smile. "Oh, my family ate it up. Cole actually tried to grab her and kiss her to shut her up, which just made us all laugh even more. We all knew it was the drugs he was on at the time."

"Really?" She turned and looked at him. She couldn't imagine it. A family laughing at the hospital while someone was injured. Last year, when her nanna had been hospitalized, her parents had shown up with the standard flowers and well wishes and then had quickly left. She was the only one who'd stayed and looked after her. After all, she felt more for the old woman than she did for both of her parents combined.

What would life have been like growing up with a crazy family, like his? She sighed and thought about it as she cooked.

"Of course, that was after we knew he was out of any danger." He shook his head and she saw his eyes go darker. "Sure, scared the hell out of us that time."

"That time?" She glanced over at him. "Were there more?"

He chuckled. "That damn kid has always been trying to kill himself. Ever since he showed up at the big house." He walked over and sat at her makeshift kitchen table. "When he got out of Lilly's car that day, it didn't take him two days to climb up into the tree house Roman and I had built a couple months earlier and fall out." He chuckled. "Course, we were egging him on. He was lucky it was only a sprained wrist that time. Then he started surfing." He shook his head again."

"About that." She stopped stirring the sauce and turned to him. "Surfing? Around here? Do the waves get big enough?"

He chuckled and shook his head. "Wakeboarding and body boarding are common enough, and you can surf during a storm, but that's about it. The first time he surfed was when we had a tropical storm. It wasn't a hurricane, but there were some big waves out there. That's when everything changed for him. He was a junior in high school. Roman and I are just a year above him. After that, he did everything he could to bum rides to where the surf was better. Started saving up his money and would fly up to the Outer Banks in North Carolina. He'd take weekend trips up there as often as he could. It was his senior year when his sponsors signed him on and the rest is history."

She smiled as she turned the burner down. "I looked him up after you told me about him." She shook her head. "Sounds like he's quite the celebrity."

"He's freaking David Beckham in water." He chuckled.

"You're pretty proud of him," she said, pouring out the water from the noodles."

"Who wouldn't be? Course, Mark and Elizabeth always hoped he'd stop trying to kill himself."

"Mark and Elizabeth?"

"Our parents." He continued talking about his family. How Julie had been an older sister to them all. How they'd lost Elizabeth, their mother, a few years back. By the time her plate was empty in front of her, she knew all about his brothers and his sister Cassey. He'd told her funny story after funny story about them growing up together. She couldn't remember ever having laughed so much, at least never during a dinner with such an attractive man.

When he talked about his family, his entire face changed. His eyes softened and even his voice grew warmer. She was mesmerized at how much he loved them.

They'd talked about family for the whole meal. She'd even opened up a little about her own parents. Well, not really, but she had mentioned that they hadn't believed her when she'd told them she was moving here and opening a shop. She did tell him about Nanna, and how it was because of her eccentric grandmother that she was here.

"She was the only Harrison to ever do what she wanted in life. Of course, she had to wait until after her husband died in a boating accident before she could go on to fulfill her dreams of becoming an actress." She smiled and rested her chin on her fist. The large windows were completely dark now, and since there were only two small bulbs in the room, the entire place looked very romantic. It had troubled her last night when she'd been sitting at the table trying to draw some sketches, but tonight, it was just perfect.

"An actress, huh?" He poured a little more wine into her glass. "Anybody I would know?"

She shrugged her shoulders. "She mainly worked on Broadway. She starred in over two dozen plays in thirty years. Of course, my parents never talk about her in polite circles." She frowned a little, remembering how embarrassed her mother had been about her own mother. She sighed. "My nanna could sure act. When I was seventeen, I snuck out to see her once. I told my parents I was staying at Whitney Jameson's house for the weekend, but instead, I drove up to New York and watched her. She was magnificent. We spent the entire weekend together, shopping, going to nightclubs, painting the town." She chuckled and rested back, remembering the great time they'd had.

"I would have loved to meet her." He leaned back and smiled at her.

She thought about what her grandmother would have thought of the hunk sitting before her. Her grandmother had always voiced her likes and dislikes in men. Marcus would have been on the like list. Then her mind turned to what kind of man her parents wanted for her and she frowned.

Why had she told him about her nanna? He'd shared his family with her and she'd wanted to share someone wonderful with him. As far as wonderful family members went, that was it. Her parents were off limits.

She shook her head. The wine was going to her head, so she pushed it aside.

"Tell me about that." She pointed to the folder they had forgotten about.

He glanced over at it and then handed it to her. "It's pretty cut and dried. If you don't like the bid, I'm sure Roman can play with the numbers a little more. I can guarantee that we're the best around. You might be able to find cheaper, but I'll warn you away from anyone who comes in too cheap. There's a serious lack of professionalism around here in contractors. I've got my hands on the best around. They will they show up when they say they will." He smiled.

She held her breath as she scanned the bid for the final price and winced just a little at the amount.

"That includes the work up here, all permits and inspections that are needed, and a two-year guarantee with all work. If something doesn't work, all you have to do is holler."

She nodded and thought about moving a few financials around to make it work. It would cut into her inventory a little, but she could always build up the stock a little slower than she'd planned.

"I think this will work. How soon can you start and how long will it take?"

"Soonest we can get the permits handled is two weeks." He frowned. "Although the city guy owes Roman a favor, so maybe that time could be cut in half. Materials and labor could be ready by then as well. Up here"—he nodded to her kitchen— "if you want anything fancy for cupboards, the time will depend on where we have to order them from. Some places take up to five weeks to deliver."

"I'd want to start downstairs first."

He nodded. "But you should pick out everything for up here, so we can have it ready by the time it's needed."

She nodded. "That's reasonable."

"Roman handles all that, so you'll be meeting with him at the office."

She arched her brows.

"He'll walk you through our distributor's website and

show you all your options. I don't really do computers."
He cleared his throat a little.

"Is that why you didn't want to see my tablet?"

He nodded. "I'm not good with electronics. I could wire up a whole office building, but when it comes to computers, I guess you could say I'm illiterate."

She smiled. "I bet you'd pick it up if you had someone to walk you through it. It's not that hard." She leaned back and looked at him. He really was handsome tonight all dressed up. She was thankful she had showered and changed before heading out to discover the area and hit the grocery store for supplies.

She loved nice things. She'd always had the best growing up, but it went beyond that. To her, it was the character of what she picked. More often than not, she veered towards the unique and less-expensive items. She'd never liked being a lemming in anything. Of course, when she lived at home, she'd had to dress as her parents had desired, which had driven her nuts.

She folded her legs under and enjoyed the way her ten-dollar skirt felt against her skin. She loved bargain hunting. Lived for it actually. Maybe that's why she'd always dreamed of opening a boutique.

He leaned on the table and she couldn't stop her eyes from traveling over his forearms. Strong, tan, and covered with a very light dusting of hair. She wondered if the rest of him would look as good.

"So, tell me something," he said, breaking into her thoughts.

She pushed them away and nodded, feeling a little twitch of fear. She was okay with telling him about her nanna, but more personal questions were off limits, at least for now.

"You mentioned that you'd come here before." She nodded, waiting for him to ask his question. "Why a boutique? I mean, it's a great location and the boardwalk could sure use something like it, but what made you want to open a shop?"

She smiled and sighed. This question was easy enough.

"When I was eleven, my parents had to go to Europe for a week and decided that dragging their preteen daughter along wasn't something they wanted to do. So, they let me stay with my nanna, who was visiting an old friend in Emerald Isle, North Carolina at the time. My nanna and her friend took me shopping and it was the first time in my childhood I could remember walking into a store where something cost under a hundred dollars." She smiled, remembering how she'd spent all of her loose change on little trinkets in the multiple stores along the shore. "For the first time in my life, I was allowed to spend my own money. I bought more useless junk that week than ten tourists." He chuckled. "It was the most fun I'd had in years."

His smile fell away. "You must not have had a very nice childhood then."

She shook her head and reached for her wine again; she felt a little more level, but she sipped it slowly. "No, not really." She looked at the dark windows. "So, when does the season officially start?" she asked, quickly changing the subject.

She was thankful when he followed along and answered, "Around Spring Break things start to really pick up. It runs all the way through the end of September if it's a good year. Although, as you may have noticed, January can be busy too."

She smiled. She loved the seasons up north but didn't think she would mind the milder changes in the south. Honestly, she was looking forward to being fairly warm year-round from here on out.

"So, you mentioned that your nanna was the only Harrison to do what she wanted, but what about you?" She looked at him without speaking. He nodded around him. "What about all this?"

He reached towards her, and for the first time that evening, she realized just how close he was to her. When his fingers brushed back a strand of hair from her face, she held her breath.

"Isn't this what you want?"

Marcus watched Shelly's pupils dilate. Her soft hazel eyes trapped him as he heard her breath hitch. He knew he was throwing her off, but she'd been throwing him off since he'd woken last night in his office to see her standing in his doorway.

"I..." she started but stopped when he ran a finger down the column of her throat. With her hair up, her slender neck had tempted him all evening. He'd daydreamed about what it would taste like if he ran his mouth over the dip at the base. His eyes traveled to her pouty lips and when her tongue darted out to them, he almost groaned out loud. "Yes, this is what I want." It came out as a whisper and for a moment, he'd forgotten what he'd asked her.

Her chair scraped as he quickly pulled her into his lap. "Tell me to stop," he said under his breath.

She shook her head from side to side and then pushed her fingers into his hair, pulling him towards her until their mouths met. He couldn't stop himself from enjoying the fullness of her lips, the softness, the taste of her.

Her fingers raked his scalp as she moved her mouth over his slowly, killing him. His own hands dug into her hips and stayed there, as he enjoyed her softness. She was light and fit perfectly in his lap. He wished that she would straddle him instead, so he could grind his want against her own.

Soft little noises came from her as he pulled her closer. He could feel her breathing hitch when he moved his hands over her hips and up her back until she was crushed against him, his chest to her softer one.

His mind whirled at the possibilities. Then he heard a buzzing and slowly pulled back until she rested her forehead on his.

"Sorry." She chuckled and shook her head. "I'd better get that." She pushed up from him and he instantly wanted her back. Her hips swayed as she walked across the room and picked up her cell phone.

"Hello?" she answered as she turned back and watched him. From twenty feet away, he could see her desire leave her when the other person started talking. She turned her back on him and started rubbing her hand over her forehead without saying a word.

He could tell that she wished he wasn't in the room, but he didn't know how to excuse himself. Besides, he didn't want to. Not yet, anyway. He wanted to make sure she was okay.

"I understand. No, this isn't… No," she said, abruptly. She was quiet for the longest time, and he thought that whoever was on the other side would need to come up for air soon. "That's not possible," she finally said, and then she clicked off her phone and set it back down on the countertop. She kept her back to him, but he could tell that she was tense.

Moving quietly, he came up behind her and laid his hands on her shoulders, causing her to jump slightly.

"Oh!" She started to turn, but he held her still.

"Don't. I can see this isn't the time, but if you need someone to talk to…" She bent her head down and he could tell she was on the verge of crying.

"No, thank you." She took a deep breath and he felt some of the tension leave her shoulders.

Gently, he turned her around and pulled her chin up with just a finger until he could see the hurt and fear in those deep eyes of hers. "If you need someone, you know where to find me. Hell, if you need anyone, Cassey or Wendy are almost always around too." He brushed his finger down her dry cheek.

She nodded and closed her eyes for a moment. "I'm sorry…"

He stopped her. "Don't be. It was a wonderful evening." He smiled and kissed those soft lips one more time. "Look over the bid and let me know if you have any questions." He waited until she nodded. "Good night, Shelly." He dropped his hands and, even though it was the hardest thing he'd ever done, he turned and walked out, leaving her hurting and alone. Just the way he knew she wanted it to be.

The cool night air did little to calm his temper.

He'd picked up enough hints during the night to know that her parents were the cause of her pain, even though she hadn't come right out and said it.

He remembered the last time he had seen his own mother and a shiver ran down his body. He knew that Shelly came from wealth. Anyone with any sense could tell. But there was more to her story than she let on. She may not own up to it, but she was running away from her family as much as she was following her dreams.

Complications. He shook his head. Why was it that all of the women worth having, came with complications?

When he opened his front door, he was shocked to see Cole standing in his living room with a black-haired beauty wrapped around him.

"Hell," he said and shut the door a little louder than needed. "Can't you get your own place?"

Cole broke away from the woman long enough to shake his head. "Why? Your place is always empty." He smiled and wrapped his arm around the slender woman. "This is Trilla. Trilla, my brother Marcus."

"Hello," she said in a thick Eastern European accent. Marcus couldn't help himself from rolling his eyes. Cole saw it and his eyebrows shot up in challenge. Biting his tongue, he shrugged his shoulders.

"How long are you staying for this time?"

Cole and Trilla walked over and sat on the sofa. His brother looked very comfortable. Trilla, not so much. "No more than a week. I hear there's a killer storm brewing off the coast of Africa."

"Killer is right." He shook his head.

"Trilla was telling me she's never been to Florida before."

"Naturally," he said under his breath.

"What was that?"

Marcus shook his head. "I suppose you'll want me to feed you?" he said instead.

"Nope, I was going to take Trilla out for a good time. We might swing by Cassey's."

Marcus laughed. "Think you'll survive this time?" His brother's eyes darkened, and he knew they were both thinking of Wendy.

"Mark my words, that woman is going to nag me to death one of these days. Maybe we'll avoid that whole scene for tonight." He tugged on Trilla's arms and pulled her up from the sofa. "Don't wait up, bro." Cole smiled, and Marcus watched them walk out together.

"Are they gone?" Roman said from his bedroom doorway.

"Damn!" Marcus jumped and spun around. "Don't do that!" He held his hand over his heart.

"Sorry." Roman laughed. "You must have known I was here. I mean, my truck is right out front." He laughed again.

Marcus shook his head. He'd been too engrossed with thoughts of Shelly to notice anything.

"Oh, well," Roman said, walking into the room. "I heard her giggling all the way up the sidewalk and locked myself in the room to avoid having to deal with another one."

"Tell me about it." He rolled his eyes.

"What do these women see in him?" Roman sat down on the sofa.

"Stars and dollar signs in his eyes," Marcus said as he reached for the remote.

"Patriots are playing tonight."

"Damn straight." He smiled and flipped it to the right channel. "And since you avoided that whole fiasco, you get to pop the corn and grab the beer." He smiled when his brother groaned but got up to do just that.

CHAPTER 7

Shelly was dirty and sweaty once again a few days later. Since she'd moved in almost a week ago, it had become standard for her to be covered in a layer of dust and grime. She had yet to unpack most of her nicest clothes since she knew they would only get ruined.

She stood back and smiled at what she'd accomplished in the last few days. The men were due to arrive first thing Tuesday to start the work downstairs, but that didn't stop her from making the upstairs a little more functional.

During one of her walks around, she'd run into a garage sale and had purchased a few items. Unfortunately, she hadn't thought ahead about dragging the items up her stairs all by herself. She could have called Marcus, but after dinner that night, she just couldn't face him. Especially since she couldn't get that kiss out of her mind.

She'd talked to him on the phone and had okayed the bid. She had kind of hoped that he would need to meet with her to have her sign papers, but he'd just informed her that he would have Roman put in for all of the permits.

Just this morning, Roman had called and informed her that all of the permits had been approved and the men would be there first thing Tuesday morning to start the work. Roman had sounded nice over the phone and she wondered when she would get to meet the rest of Marcus's family.

Dusting off her hands, she decided a shower and dinner at Cassey's sounded better than eating all by herself. She opened one of the boxes that held her nicer clothes and put on a pair of silver tights with her white sweater skirt. When she pulled out her favorite pair of heeled boots, she sighed. She missed wearing her nice things. Soon, she promised herself. Soon, she would have her whole wardrobe back again.

She put on some silver hoops and bracelets, finished curling her hair, and applied just the right amount of gloss to her lips. She felt regenerated.

Locking up, she walked a little too fast down the boardwalk towards the bar and grill. It was just past eight when she walked in and waved at Wendy behind the bar. She'd visited with her and Cassey several times that week. The two of them had stopped by one day to check up on her and see if she needed any help. At the time, she hadn't but could have used one or both of them earlier that day hauling up the nightstands and shelves she'd purchased.

"There you are." Wendy smiled at her. "I was just talking about you." She nodded to another woman who sat at the bar. "This is Rosa. She runs Rosa's Coffee shop down the street."

"Hello." Shelly shook the shorter woman's hand. "Nice to meet you. I stopped by your business just yesterday." She smiled.

"Oh, I hope you enjoyed?"

Shelly sat down next to her. "Yes, very much."

"Are you having dinner?" Wendy asked, and when she nodded, she handed her a menu. "Anything to drink?"

"Hmm." She looked up at the menu, "I'm in the mood for a beer." She smiled. "Blue Moon with an orange, please."

Wendy nodded and moved off to get her order.

"Wendy was telling me you're going to open a boutique?"

"Yes, if all goes well. Construction starts on Tuesday."

"Oh, how exciting."

Shelly laughed. "I can't wait."

"If you need anything, let me know. It may not look like it but finding good help around here during the off-season is hard."

"Oh?" Shelly leaned closer.

Rosa nodded. "Local kids are spoiled." She shook her head. "I have the names of a few good people I can pass to you. Some I still employ; some want different kinds of jobs." Rosa took another sip of her beer. "Actually, I think I might know someone who's perfect." She tilted her head. "Will you hire full time or part time?"

"Well, to begin with, part-time. I think." She laughed. "I hadn't even thought that far ahead."

By the time her food arrived, Rosa had given her advice on several aspects of running a business Shelly hadn't even thought about. She was writing a list of things she needed to add to her other lists on a napkin.

When Rosa moved to leave, Shelly shook her hand. "I can't thank you enough for helping me."

Rosa smiled. "My pleasure. If you have any questions…here." She handed her a card.

"Wow," she said to Wendy after Rosa left, "am I glad I came in tonight."

Wendy smiled. "Rosa doesn't just own the coffee shop down the way."

"Oh?"

Wendy leaned on the bar and shook her head. "Have you heard of Breegee's?"

"The coffee company?"

Wendy nodded. "You just met Rosa Breegee herself. Queen of the coffee bean."

"What?" Shelly looked off towards the door, but the small woman had already disappeared.

"That woman is richer than God." Wendy sighed. "But still has a good head on her shoulders."

"I can't believe I was taking advice from someone who runs a multibillion-dollar company."

"And a local coffee shop." Wendy smiled and walked away to take someone else's order.

Shelly shook her head and finished off her beer. She was about to order another one when she saw Wendy stiffen and frown. Her friend's eyes turned to ice. Shelly glanced over to see what could have caused such a reaction and noticed a very good-looking couple walk in.

The woman looked vaguely familiar to her and could have easily stepped from the pages of Sports Illustrated. The man, from GQ. Then she took another look at the man and realization dawned. This was Cole. Marcus's brother. She glanced back at Wendy and couldn't help but smile just a little. She wondered if the woman knew she had it bad. From the outside, she looked pissed. Beyond pissed. If the lighting was just right, she would have wagered she would see steam coming off Wendy's skin. But Shelly could see the longing in her blue eyes. Longing and hurt.

Shelly walked over and broke Wendy's view. "Is everything okay?"

Wendy blinked a few times and then nodded. "Sure." She shook her head. "Just same ol' stuff. Did you want another beer?" she asked just as the couple walked up to the bar.

Wendy didn't even spare them a glance, "You still hanging around? Don't you have to go kill yourself in Africa?" When she didn't get a response, she looked up at the couple. Cole was frowning. The woman, on the other hand, was all smiles.

Shelly doubted the woman knew how to frown. Maybe she'd had too much plastic surgery.

"Plans changed, we're heading out tomorrow. I thought I'd come in and say bye to Cassey." He glanced around the room. "Is she…"

"Upstairs," Wendy said, setting another beer in front of Shelly. "This is Shelly. She's going to open a boutique on the boardwalk."

Cole glanced her way. His eyes caught hers and she saw his instant attraction in them. His smile was slow and, she had to admit, breathtaking.

"Sure." He dropped the dark-haired woman's hand and walked over to take hers to his lips. "My pleasure." His hand was tan and warm. She glanced back at the beauty behind him and she could tell the woman was used to him flirting. She had to admit he was smooth.

"Your brother Marcus has told me so much about you."

"Oh?" His blonde eyebrows shot up. "Only believe the good stuff." He winked.

She smiled.

"He's supposed to be meeting us here after the game. Roman, too." He glanced around again. "I guess we're a little early." He dropped her hand and sat next to her. The other woman sat on the other side of him, no doubt not wanting to be too far away from her mark.

"This is Trilla." He nodded between them. He grabbed Wendy's hand as she rushed by. "I'll have my usual."

Shelly watched with some humor as Wendy yanked her hand away and glared at the woman. "You?"

"Oh, a spritzer water with lime, please." Shelly couldn't quite pinpoint the accent.

Wendy nodded and marched off to get the drinks.

"So, you moved down here from…" He left the question hanging. When she turned to him, she realized he'd turned his entire body towards her, leaving his girlfriend at his back and ignored.

"DC," she answered, not really thinking.

"Oh?" He glanced at Wendy as she set his drink in front of him. "I had heard it was Boston." Instantly, her cheeks turned red and she glanced at Wendy who just smiled at her.

"By way of Boston," she recovered.

"Other than opening your own business, what brings you down to our humble shores?" He leaned on the bar, looking quite comfortable as he sipped the clear drink.

"The sand and beaches." She smiled. "Is there any other reason needed?"

He smiled back at her and lifted his glass in a toast. "Surf." When he smiled, she noticed small dimples on either side of his mouth. No one should be this good at flirting. She was way out of her league.

"So, what do you do, Trilla?" She glanced around Cole towards the woman, who was trying to pout but ended up looking like she was smiling for a teeth-whitening commercial instead.

"I'm a model." She ran off a list of clothing lines that Shelly was all too familiar with, and instantly she knew where she'd seen her before. And it wasn't in any magazine.

Tyler. Her heart skipped a few beats. Please, God, don't let her recognize me. She was thankful when no recognition crossed the woman's eyes and relaxed a little.

"How wonderful," she said quickly and leaned back so the woman couldn't get a better look at her.

"There they are," Cole said, turning around and standing up. "Thought you two had gotten lost."

Shelly turned around and saw Marcus and another dark-haired man walk in and hug their brother. She didn't think it possible, but Roman was even better looking than Cole. Then her eyes fell on Marcus, and it was impossible to break away. She watched the brothers walking towards her with the dying sun behind them and her breath caught. If only she had a camera to capture all the beauty.

"Hi." Marcus walked over to her and placed a soft kiss on her lips, no doubt staking his claim for his brothers to see. She couldn't stop herself from smiling.

"Hi, right back."

"I'm glad you're here. We were just sending this guy off again." He nodded to Cole.

"Yes, so I hear."

"You two met?" He frowned a little.

"About two minutes before you walked in." She smiled and saw him relax a little.

"This must be Shelly." Roman walked over and took her hand away from Marcus's and shook it lightly.

"And you're Roman." She smiled.

"Guilty. It's good to finally meet you."

"Boys?" Wendy interrupted. "Your usual?"

The two nodded. "Here's your sister and soon to be brother-in-law now." Wendy nodded towards the stairs.

Shelly watched Cassey walk down the back stairs with a good-looking man.

"That's Luke, my sister's fiancé," Marcus whispered in her ear. "He owns the new hotel just outside of town." She'd seen the large resort-like hotel and knew that Marcus and Roman's construction company had done all the work.

After the introductions were made, they moved over to a large booth near the back of the room. She hadn't meant to be dragged along, but Marcus had taken her hand and she couldn't help but follow.

At first, she felt like an outsider in the group, but by the time everyone's food had arrived, she was starting to feel more comfortable. She found herself laughing at the jokes and stories everyone was telling.

Marcus ordered her a very large, very delicious piece of key lime pie after he found out that she'd already eaten. She had to admit, it was the best time she'd had in a long while.

It was killing Marcus to watch her. He'd seen both Roman

and Cole eyeing Shelly as she nibbled—a little too seductively—on that pie. He was just thankful they were sitting in a large booth, or he would have been tempted to go over there and knock his brother's heads together for staring at her so.

Then again, he too found it hard to concentrate on the conversation.

He wanted to taste those lips of hers again but had to settle for reaching under the table and holding her hand instead. He half-heartedly listened to his family talk about good old times and chuckled at some of the stories. He joined in the storytelling, making sure to add some of his siblings' most embarrassing moments into the mix. But his mind kept wandering back to getting Shelly alone.

Finally, Cole stood up and excused himself and his latest catch, claiming their flight left early and they had to get some rest. Marcus knew that his brother had more than sleep on his mind.

Shortly after, Cassey and Luke disappeared as well, but he knew that his sister wouldn't call it quits for the night, either.

He squeezed Shelly's hand and whispered close to her ear, "What do you say to a walk on the beach?"

She smiled and nodded, and he felt his heart skip just thinking about being alone with her again.

They excused themselves and he took her hand as they stepped outside. The evening air was a little chilly, but at least the wind that had caused havoc earlier that day at a job site had died down. He smiled when he saw that she'd worn a light jacket.

"You're learning." He nodded.

She smiled. "It was downright cold earlier today."

"Yeah, we get a handful of days like that during the winter. Still, I'd take them over five feet of snow any day."

She laughed. "I don't know, there's something nice about a fresh layer of powder." She moved closer to him and rested her arm through his as they walked. "Being stuck in the house, watching it fall at night." She sighed. They stopped to remove their shoes at the bottom of the boardwalk steps and walked out onto the still-warm sand. "Then again, I don't think any amount of snow could be better than warm, soft sand on your feet."

He chuckled. "Living on the best beach on the Gulf does have its perks. Are you ready for the work to start next week?"

"Boy, am I!" She laughed. "I went over some changes with your brother over the phone. Did he mention them?" She glanced at him. Since the sun had gone down almost two hours earlier, the beach was fairly dark. But he could still see her face clearly enough from the lights on the boardwalk.

"Yeah." He nodded. "He mentioned you wanted a bigger area in the back."

She nodded and looked embarrassed. "I wanted some room to work on my own designs."

"Designs? As in clothing?" He stopped and looked at her.

She nodded. "I took a few classes." She laughed. "Actually, more than a few. Most of them my parents didn't know about. If they knew…" She sighed and looked off towards the water.

"I bet you're great at it." He took her hand in his and started walking again.

She smiled again. "Roman emailed me the changes and I really liked them."

He nodded. "What did you think of my family?"

She laughed again. "They're wonderful. I can't believe how funny you all are together."

"Yeah, growing up we never really had any dull moments." He smiled and tugged on her hand until she stopped. "They liked you." He brushed a long strand of her hair away from her face. Since it was soft and smelled so good, he kept his fingers tangled in the light tresses.

"How can you tell?" she asked softly.

"I have my ways." He stepped closer to her and felt her warmth next to him. "I'm in complete agreement with them."

"Oh?" She wrapped her arms around his shoulders, which pushed her chest up against his nicely. He nodded, feeling his mouth go dry.

The kiss was soft and sweet, which left him shaking even more.

"I like you as well." He heard a "but" before she even said it. "But"—she pushed back just a little— "I'm not sure if I'm ready to explore anything more than this. At the moment." She looked down at their joined hands.

He released the breath he'd been holding and smiled down at her. "This… is good." When her eyes moved up to his, he saw confusion.

"I mean…"

He chuckled, stopping her. "I know what you meant." He pulled her close again. "I don't mind taking this slow."

Almost an hour later, after he'd walked her back to her place, he strolled into his apartment to find Cole getting yelled at by his girl. He stopped in the doorway, wishing he'd heard the fight before he'd opened the door. Backing out was no longer an option. His brother silently pleaded with him not to leave from across the room.

It was just past one o'clock when he finally got to settle down for the night, which sucked because he had to be on a job before sunrise the next morning. Not to mention that he was supposed to drop his brother off at the airport as well. And now that it was clear that his brother was going to Africa alone, he wasn't looking forward to the mood Cole was going to be in during the short drive either.

CHAPTER 8

Marcus usually loved his work, but he just couldn't concentrate on it for the next few days. He kept thinking about Shelly's project and itched to get his hands on her apartment. The store was going to be a challenge for him as well, but there was just something about turning a big open space into a place she would live in and enjoy.

He'd called Susan Robinson—the best Realtor around—and asked her to keep an eye out for a place for him. She was an old high school flame, but now she had a house full of kids and a lawyer husband.

Susan had quickly printed him out a list of places that matched his requirements.

He didn't tell his brother about the listings. He went through the list on his own, one house at a time.

He found a few that he put on his "maybe" list, but so far, nothing had jumped out at him.

When the weekend came along, he knocked out every house on the list. He thought he'd found the one. He tried like crazy to stay away from Shelly since he knew she wanted to take their relationship slowly. He really didn't mind. He thought of women like he thought of a really good remodeling project—when a project was worth working on, it didn't matter to him how long it took to complete. What he enjoyed was building it up, working on each little project, and finally getting the rewards at the end.

He'd had a few relationships that had been worth the effort over the years. None of them had lasted long, but all of them had been worth the wait. He knew Shelly would be worth it and actually enjoyed taking his time with her.

From the hints he'd gotten from her, she wasn't too keen on her family. He knew what it was like to have an unstable family life. Hell, he'd lived it for years with his real mother.

He couldn't imagine what life would have been like without the Graytons. Not everyone was lucky enough to have as much love as they'd gotten in that old house.

It was early Sunday morning and he had a list of open houses Susan wanted him to go to. Even though he'd driven by most of the homes on her list already, he'd yet to see the inside of a few of them and she thought it would make a difference.

For some reason, he found himself heading down to Shelly's place beforehand. He stood at the bottom of her steps for ten minutes, trying to figure out what he was doing there.

When he felt a light tap on his shoulder, he spun around to see her standing there, laughing at him.

"Well, were you just going to stand here all day, frowning at your feet?" She smiled up at him.

"Hmmm?" He shook his head a few times. "What?"

She laughed again. "You've been standing here for a while. I noticed you when I came out of the Lunch Box," She motioned down the walkway to where the diner sat. "I thought maybe you were going to go up, but you just kept looking at your feet."

He frowned. Had he been? Why hadn't he gone up the stairs yet? He knew the reason but didn't want to tell her. His cheeks must have turned a little red because her smile faltered.

"Is something wrong?"

When he shook his head no, she continued to look at him.

"I…" He blinked a few times. "I'm heading out to look at some places. You know, to remodel. I was wondering…" He dropped off, feeling like a fool.

"Oh, you're going to buy a home and rebuild it?" The look on her face helped ease his mind a little. He had worried she would find it dull and boring, which would have put him off a little in their relationship.

He felt like a fool for not telling her the house was for him, not to fix up and make a profit from.

"I'd love to go with you if you're asking." She smiled again, and he almost forgot to breathe. The sunlight was catching the highlights in her hair, making it glow. He wanted to reach out and touch the softness but stuck his hands in his pocket instead. Best not to go too fast.

"Great. Good." He cleared his throat and started to turn around.

"Have you had breakfast?" she asked as she caught up with him.

He nodded. "I just had some of the best cinnamon rolls."

He chuckled. "Yeah, I try to only have Lunch Box's cinnamon rolls once a year." He smiled. "They're the best, but if I didn't pace myself, I'd eat them every day and end up fat and slow."

She reached over and took his hand, almost causing his steps to falter.

"I know what you mean." She sighed. "I'm already dreaming of another, and I just finished eating two of them." She laughed holding onto her stomach. A few extra pounds on her wouldn't be such a bad thing, he thought. It wasn't as if she was *skinny* skinny, but he'd gotten his hands around her and knew that she could handle a little more.

He liked women in all shapes and sizes, as long as they were soft and made him laugh. He smiled at her as he opened his car door for her.

When he got in beside her, she turned to him. "So, where are we off to first?"

He handed her a list of homes. "Pick one. The highlighted ones have open houses today."

"Oh." She sounded excited. "I've always wanted to go to an open house." She looked over the list. "There's one just a few blocks from here; let's start with that one."

He knew the place she was talking about. "Yeah, this is one of the ones on my second list," he said as he pulled out of his parking spot.

"Second list?" She clicked her seat belt into place.

"I drove by all of them this week. The ones with an X next to them are off the list. Ones with a check are on my second list, meaning I'd like to see the inside before I narrow the field down."

She glanced at the list again.

"You have twelve homes on your second list." She smiled over at him.

"Wow, that many?" He shook his head. "I thought I'd narrowed it down more."

"Well, nine of them have open houses today," she said after looking at his list again. "Maybe I can help you narrow them down further."

He nodded. "I'd appreciate the help."

She set the list down between them. "So, what are you looking for?"

He thought about it. At one point, he'd known exactly what he wanted in a house. But so much had changed in the years since he'd initially built the list in his mind. "It has to have at least four bedrooms and three baths."

"Beach front, bay front, or don't you care?"

He shrugged his shoulders. "Don't care, as long as it has a good-sized yard. I don't like places that sit right on top of one another." He frowned. "Most of those places I already crossed off the list."

"Okay." She nodded. "Garage?"

He nodded. "I have a lot of tools and need the storage. I think I handled that in the first round, too." He thought about what else he'd want in a place. "I prefer a fixer-upper. Something I could put my own touches into. Course, I don't want to have to demolish the place and start from scratch."

She nodded again as they stopped in front of the first house.

"Oh, this is lovely." She undid her seat belt and leaned

forward. "It's right off the main road, though. During tourist season, you might hear a lot of traffic."

He hadn't thought about that and mentally started to scratch it off the list.

"But let's go inside. Maybe the inside will charm you further." She smiled over at him and he realized he didn't care if he wasted time on a house he wasn't going to buy since she was there.

The place was a bust. He knew it the second he walked in and saw that it had been recently renovated. He was happy when Shelly quickly walked through the place.

As they drove away, she put an X by the listing. "I can't believe they wanted that much for that place." She frowned. "Are any of these listings in your price range?"

He nodded. "Yeah, I had a friend print these up for me. They're all at least four bedrooms, three baths, with a garage and in my price range. That place would have maxed out my budget and now I know why." He shook his head. "Some people should never do home projects themselves."

She laughed. "I'm so happy you said that. Did you see what color they painted the walls?" She gasped and leaned back. "I'm going to be seeing that color of green all day now."

He chuckled and nodded. "Where's the next one?"

She rattled off an address on Sugar Sand Lane and he turned the truck in that direction. This was one of the places he really liked. It was on a side road that was a dead end, so the chances of having a lot of traffic were slim. There wasn't any direct beach access, but the place was on a small hill so it overlooked the water just the same.

When they parked in front, she leaned forward and sighed.

"It's gorgeous."

He nodded. "My thoughts as well. Hopefully, the inside isn't too bad. If I remember correctly, the price was a little low." He frowned and looked at the listing. "Yeah, really low for this area."

"Well, let's go find out why." She smiled and jumped down from his truck.

When they walked into the place, Marcus knew he'd found what he'd been looking for. The place needed a lot of work. Its structure was good, but everything from the flooring to the gaudy ceiling fans needed to be replaced.

"Hmmm," she said as they walked into the master bathroom. "Maybe you could yank everything out and put in a nice Jacuzzi tub, shower combo over there."

He smiled. "My thoughts exactly."

As they went room to room, she voiced her opinions and he found it very exciting that they matched with his own thoughts.

When they walked out onto the back deck, they both sighed. "This makes the place worth all the work." She leaned on the post and sighed again. "I mean, can you imagine sitting out here every evening and having a cold beer, watching the sunset?"

He must have been quiet too long because she glanced over at him and frowned. "What?" she asked, turning towards him.

He shook his head. "It's like you're reading my mind." He smiled.

"Well, now we know why the price is low. There's a lot to do, but I think it could be great."

He nodded again.

"The question is, is it too much for you?"

He stepped closer to her. "You keep asking me that. Nothing is too much for me." He dipped his head and kissed her lightly. "Thanks for coming with me."

She pulled back a little. "Don't you want to look at the other houses?"

He shook his head no. "I know when I've spotted something I want." He smiled at her. "Even if it means waiting and working a little harder for it."

He watched realization cross her eyes, then her cheeks flooded with heat. When she smiled a little, he knew he'd been right about her. She was going to be worth the wait.

Shelly sat in the truck in silence. She couldn't get over how sure he was. Not only about the property, but about her.

She really did enjoy spending time with him. But she didn't like rushing into relationships. Especially since she'd known him for such a short time. But he'd made it very clear that he was willing to wait, to work on the relationship.

She shook her head and looked out the window. Relationship. That was a word she usually cringed at. Relationships hadn't necessarily worked out for her in the past.

She really did like looking at the homes with him. It was hard not to dream about someday buying her own home. But when it came to having her own family, that's where she usually stopped dreaming.

Ever since she was a little girl, she'd always known

she didn't want children. Not that she didn't like them, but she didn't want to chance to become a parent like she'd had growing up. Or for that matter, any that she had known in her childhood.

Even her nanna had told her that she'd been a terrible mother to her own child. Shelly's mother had been an only child and her nanna had told her that was because she'd realized shortly after her daughter had been born that she wasn't cut out to be a mother.

"Well, since we have the rest of the day off, how would you like to swing by my folks' place? I'm supposed to drop some stuff off to my old man." He nodded to a large box that sat in the bed of his truck. "I've been driving that thing around for almost a week now."

"Do they live far?" she asked.

"The other side of the bay. It's about a twenty-minute drive."

She nodded. "I've got nothing better to do until your crew arrives on Tuesday." She smiled thinking that a drive would be nice. She hadn't really had a chance to see much of the area yet. She'd been planning to go exploring this weekend but had gotten caught up in planning out her business.

"My mother, Elizabeth, passed away a few years back."

"Oh, I'm sorry."

"Dad..." He shook his head and chuckled. "Mark is still going strong." He laughed. "I remember thinking how frail he looked so many years ago when I first saw him. Hell, if he doesn't look just the same now, though."

She smiled. "You said something about an older sister?"

He nodded. "Julie still lives there. She retired from teaching a few years back and just opened some of the rooms up as a kind of bed and breakfast." He chuckled again. "I'll prepare you now. She's a… free spirit." He smiled over at her and her eyebrows shot up. He shook his head. "You'll see. I think you'll like her," he said as they drove over the long bridge that would lead them to the other side of the bay.

"It must have been nice growing up so close to the beach."

He nodded. "Course, we used to spend more time in the bay than anything. Everyone except Cole, that is. We had a little boat that we'd go out fishing in. We would always spend weekends camping out, trying to see who could catch the biggest fish."

She smiled. "Sounds like you had a wonderful childhood."

He nodded and then glanced over at her. "Living with the Graytons was the best thing that ever happened to me. To all of us." He shook his head and watched the road as it turned.

He was silent for a while, but when he turned off the main road, he glanced over at her and asked. "What about you?"

"Me?" She watched the scenery go by. She'd been thinking about her childhood, how everything had changed.

"Sure. I can tell you don't want to talk about your folks, but surely you had some good times?"

She nodded and then turned to him when she realized he was paying attention to driving and not looking at her. "I guess I had the standard good times." She shrugged her shoulders.

"Was it your folks?" he asked, and she knew what he was asking.

"Yes and no." She looked off as they rounded another road. "They both had such high-powered jobs and when my father…" She sighed. "Let's just say his current job takes precedence over family life."

"No job should come before your family," he said, frowning over at her.

"I agree, but Daddy doesn't see it that way, and neither did my mother." He slowed down for a tight curve.

"What exactly does your father do?" he asked as they turned off the road and hit a dirt driveway. She was so busy looking at the wonderful old house in front of her, she didn't focus on her answer.

"He's a politician," she said absentmindedly as she took in the beautiful house. "Oh! This is wonderful." She smiled and looked over at him. If she had been paying attention, she would have seen his slight frown as he stopped the truck. "I can't believe you grew up here." She jumped out of the truck and tried to take everything in.

The house was a huge three-story Victorian, painted a light shade of blue. The front porch was massive and ran the whole length of the place. The windows gleamed in the sunlight.

"It's just like in a fairy tale," she said, turning to him.

He chuckled. "It's a nightmare to paint."

She shook her head. "It's wonderful."

"Well, come on." He took her hand and led her to the front porch. Julie was standing in the doorway, smiling at them when they walked up.

"Hi." She nodded to Shelly when they stood in front of her.

Shelly could see what Marcus meant about his sister. She had long dark hair that was parted in the middle. She wore a loose dress with a flower pattern on it. She wasn't wearing any shoes or socks and it looked to Shelly like the woman was used to going barefoot. Marcus walked over and gave the woman a hug.

"Julie, this is Shelly Harrison. She's opening shop a couple doors down from Cassey."

Julie nodded again. "It's so wonderful to meet you. I've heard lots about you from Cassey." Julie gave Marcus a stern look, which quickly disappeared when Marcus smiled. "Well, come on in. I was just making some lunch. I have guests, so we won't be eating alone."

Julie's guests were a nice couple from New York who were visiting Florida for the first time. The young couple not only looked very much in love but very anxious to be off spending time to themselves.

She met Mark Grayton, the man Marcus called dad. To say the man was frail was an understatement. Shelly thought he looked weaker than her grandmother had just before she'd passed away. But Marcus had told her that he'd always looked that way. Mr. Grayton seemed like a good man. He shook her hand and cracked a joke, making her laugh as they sat down for lunch in a large dining room.

They ate sandwiches and some wonderful homemade chicken soup as Marcus and his family chatted and joked with Julie's guests.

"We've decided to go paragliding, today," Julie's guest Steve blurted out as he reached over and took his girlfriend

Lori's hand in his. "We've never been. Can you recommend someplace to go?" he asked Marcus.

Marcus chuckled. "Never been myself, but I hear Sea Breeze is good. They've been in business for as long as I can remember. They have a little booth set up in Sea Side. You can't miss it."

"Thanks," Steve said again and squeezed his girlfriend's hand.

After lunch, the young couple took off, no doubt heading to the beach. Marcus and his father went out to unload the items from his truck that he'd come to deliver while Shelly helped Julie clear the table.

"It was wonderful to meet you," Julie said, taking the dishes from Shelly. "It's been a while since Marcus has brought anyone home." Julie smiled at her.

Shelly instantly felt like she should explain. "Oh, Marcus is such a good friend." Just hearing the words come from her mouth made her cringe.

Julie chuckled when she saw it. "Marcus is many things."

Shelly nodded and decided to keep her mouth shut for the rest of the day.

"Cassey and Roman think the world of you."

"Oh?" Shelly couldn't help it, she smiled. "I simply adore them both. Cassey is such an inspiration and Roman too, with his home for children."

Julie nodded. "It's so wonderful seeing how far they've all come." Julie turned away from the messy sink. "I can clean this up later. Let's go sit out on the porch since it's such a nice day."

Shelly nodded and followed her outside. Marcus and his father were done unloading the large box from his truck, and she could hear them out in the garage banging on something.

"Those two always disappear out to the workshop." Julie chuckled.

"You have a beautiful home," Shelly said sitting down next to Julie on a large swing.

"Thank you. We owe its beauty to Marcus and Roman." She smiled. "When they first came to us, the house was in bad shape. Marcus was always looking for something to do around here." She shook her head and then took a sip of her drink.

Shelly smiled. "We drove around looking for houses today for him to fix up."

Julie laughed and nodded. "That boy loves to stay busy." Her smile faltered. "He never did like sitting still for too long." She shook her head.

"He mentioned needing a vacation."

Julie laughed. "The moment that boy takes a real vacation, you let me know because then I'll know hell has frozen over."

Shelly frowned a little.

"Of course, there was that time he broke his wrist." Julie chuckled. "'Bout near killed him not being able to fix anything."

"How did he break it?" Shelly asked, sitting back to listen.

"Well, that was the summer Roman and Marcus decided that anyone could do what Cole did. Surfing and bodyboarding like he does." Julie looked at her to make sure she understood, so Shelly nodded for her to continue. "Marcus took the skim board and the first time he tossed it down and jumped on it, his feet flew one way and his body the other." She chuckled again. "Landed on his wrist with a snap. He never tried boarding again."

Shelly shook her head. "I'm not big on sports, either. I was in dance for a few years, but I could never get the hang of anything else."

"My sister Karen was the one that was always good at everything." Julie looked off towards the garage as a loud noise came from there. There was a burst of laughter and she smiled. "That boy saved him. He saved us all, really."

Shelly waited, watching Julie who shook her head as the smile faded.

"I haven't told anyone else this"—Julie looked towards her— "but I had a son about Marcus's age. Stephan died less than a year before Marcus came to us." Julie's eyes looked so sad. "Dad and I took it the hardest." She smiled when a new burst of loud laughter came from the open garage doors. "I don't even think any of the kids knew about Stephan."

"Why not?" Shelly left the question hanging.

Julie shrugged her shoulders. "No real reason. Each of the kids was going through their own personal hell, as were we. We didn't ask them about their lives." She shrugged again. "We didn't talk about ours."

Just then the men walked out of the garage. Marcus's arm was slung over the older man's shoulders in a loving manner. They looked good together, like they belonged, making Shelly wish that she would experience something like it, at least once in her life.

arcus could tell that Shelly was thinking on the drive back home. Her eyes were a little misty and she kept them trained out the side window instead of straight ahead.

"Did Julie say something to upset you?" he asked as they started driving over the bay bridge.

"No." She shook her head. "She's a wonderful woman. I like them both." She smiled over at him.

When they'd crossed the bridge, he pulled off onto a side road and went to one of his favorite hidden fishing spots and parked. Here there was no traffic, no noise to take his attention off of the conversation he wanted.

"Shelly?" He punched the button releasing his seat belt and turned towards her. "Something is bothering you. Talk to me."

She sighed and closed her eyes for a moment. He sat there waiting.

"I…" she started, but then shook her head before she continued. "As you have probably guessed, I didn't have a great family growing up. As I mentioned, my parents were too involved in their careers to bother with raising their daughter. Not until I hit my teens did I finally realize that I was just a tool to them. Something to be used when they needed a family photo opportunity for an event. They dragged me to charity events to boost my father's career." She closed her eyes again and he could tell she was struggling with the pain.

"Your dad is Congressmen Gerald Harrison, isn't he?" He watched her flinch at her father's name and then her eyes met his and he could see even more pain.

"Yes." She looked down at her hands. "The only time he was around when I was growing up was when there were news cameras watching." She sighed. "To my mother, I was someone who prevented her from being the socialite she needed to be to further her husband's career."

He reached over and took her hand in his, scooting closer to her. She glanced over at him. He thought there would be tears in her eyes. Instead, there was just a dull, empty look. He could tell that years of pain had taken their toll on her and doubted that she cried anymore about the pain her parents had caused.

"It got to the point that I was just going along with everything they demanded. Everything they wanted. Then one day, the day that Nanna died, something snapped, and I woke up. I'd always dreamed about coming back here, to my someday beach, of opening a shop, of living here forever." She looked at him. "I bought my building and shortly after, I packed everything I could and jumped in my car and didn't stop until I was here." She smiled.

He smiled at her. "You're a strong person." He pulled her close and placed a kiss on the top of her head.

"I don't know about that. I didn't lie when I said that I'd told my parents about moving here, about opening my own shop." She pulled away a little and looked up at him. "But the fact is, I didn't really tell them face-to-face. I left them a voicemail. Then, the other day, my mother called and told me that the joke was over and it was time for me to come home. Do you know, they actually think I'm just down here on vacation?" She laughed bitterly.

"What did you tell them?" He played with a strand of her hair that had fallen over his hand.

She sighed. "I told her that I wasn't going back to school. That I'd officially dropped out and was opening my own shop here and nothing they could say or do would make me change my mind."

"And?" He waited, holding his breath.

She laughed. "She told me that she was too busy to continue this pointless conversation since she had just arrived at the country club and was meeting several women for lunch. Then she told me to call her back later this week after I'd come to my senses."

He shook his head in disbelief.

"So, what made you sad today? Did my aunt say something to upset you?"

She looked up at him and shook her head no. "It was just… seeing you, with them. So happy together." She sighed.

He smiled. "My family has plenty of room in their hearts." He pulled her closer and placed a gentle kiss on those soft lips. He felt the quick punch of desire but pushed it towards the back, knowing that it wasn't what she needed at the moment.

When she pulled away a little, he was happy to see that

her eyes were back to shining. Then she frowned a little. "Did you know that your aunt had a son your age that died?"

He nodded. "I found out shortly after I arrived there. Why?"

She shook her head and smiled a little. "She told me that you saved them all. But from hearing you talk, they saved you."

He smiled and nodded. "It was a mutual rescue."

She chuckled and then sobered a little. "How did Stephan die?"

"Car accident. Took him and his father at once." He shook his head. "About a week after I got there, I found a picture of them along with the newspaper article." He frowned and dropped his hand. "The first two months of being there, I watched my sisters change, become happier."

She smiled up at him. "They were very lucky to find you."

He shook his head. "I was the lucky one." He sighed. "What do you say to starting your project a little early?"

Her eyebrows shot up. "I thought—"

"Since I'm the boss, I can set the schedule," he interrupted her. "Besides, I feel like pounding something with a sledgehammer. What about you?"

She smiled. "Sounds fun. What shall we bang on and destroy?"

He laughed. "I was thinking of starting on the back wall that needs to come down. But first, a stop off at my place to get some tools."

After he'd piled a few tools he knew they would need in the back of his truck, they headed back to her shop. She let him in and he got to work making sure the power and water were off on that level while she raced upstairs to change.

When she came back down in her work clothes, he handed her a sledgehammer, gloves, and some protective glasses. "Ready?" He picked up his own hammer and stood a few feet away from her.

"I've never done this before. Do I just…"

He laughed. "You can over think this. Just swing and hit something. Oh, make sure to use full swings. I don't want to see any girlie stuff here." He smiled at her.

"Girlie?" She frowned. "I don't do girlie things." She pouted a little.

He laughed. "Prove it. On the count of three?" She nodded, and he counted and swung with her. He was impressed. She may have never done this before, but she put everything she had into each swing.

It took them a little under an hour to have the back wall knocked out.

"That felt good." She smiled over at him and he could see a slight sheen of sweat on her brow. "What else needs destroying?" She looked around.

"Hang on, Xena." He laughed. "Part of destroying is cleaning up." He nodded to the huge pile of boards and drywall that sat at their feet. "We've got to haul all this out to that dumpster we delivered on Friday." She frowned a little, but then she set her sledgehammer down and pulled the wheelbarrow closer so they could load it up.

He had never dated a woman that didn't complain when hard work was required. Shelly was the exception to the rule. She poured one hundred percent into everything she did. By the time the mess was completely gone, they were both covered in dust, dirt, and sweat.

It totally shocked him that she still had a smile on her face. She'd tied her hair up in a braid, and some of it had escaped falling around her face. She looked at him and he felt something shift inside, something that he had never felt before. It took his breath away and he was speechless for almost an entire minute.

"Is everything okay?" she asked, looking at him funny.

All he could do was nod his head. He tried to look away from her, but she was standing in the fading light of the big windows with the setting sun behind her. She was the most beautiful thing he'd ever seen. Even covered in grime, she was beautiful.

Then she walked towards him slowly and he lost the rest of his breath as he watched her move. Her hips swayed in the tight jeans she was wearing. Even the large shirt she'd thrown on looked very appealing.

She didn't stop walking until she bumped into his chest with hers. Then her arms wrapped around his shoulders and he couldn't stop his hands from going to her hips, pulling her closer.

"I just can't seem to stop wanting this," she said before she stood up on her toes and placed her lips against his.

Shelly's hands shook as she tugged on his hair to bring his lips down to hers. She'd witnessed his eyes heat from across the room and knew his mood had changed. She couldn't stop her body from responding to his as his fingers dug into her hips. She wanted him and instantly felt torn.

She'd never gotten this close to someone before. Never dreamed it was possible.

When his mouth moved over hers, she sighed and enjoyed the warmth that spread down to her toes. Then he took a step closer, backing her up until her shoulders came up against the outer wall. She ached and arched as his hands ran over her, tugging and pulling her large T-shirt out of her old jeans until, finally, she felt his callused hands on her bare skin. She moaned with pleasure as her body responded to his touch.

When his head dipped, and his mouth spread over her exposed skin, she closed her eyes and sighed at the wonderful feeling of his hot lips on her breast.

Years, it had been years since she'd felt anything like this. She shook her head. She'd never felt anything as wonderful as Marcus's mouth on her. His tongue played over her, causing little bumps to raise up everywhere.

Her fingers were tangled in his hair, pulling him closer as he moaned and enjoyed the taste of her. She realized she was completely sweaty and probably covered in dust, but he didn't seem to mind. Instead, he lapped at her like she was the best tasting cream he'd ever experienced.

She pushed her hips towards him and moaned again as his fingers brushed across her lower belly. Shivers raced through her as his finger dipped just below her jeans.

"Please," she begged, not really caring if she sounded desperate.

Her mind kept screaming at her to stop, that this was all too soon. But her body was so heated from his touch that everything else fell away.

"Marcus, please," she begged again, not sure of what she was asking. All she knew was that he was touching her like she was a piece of glass. So gentle. Couldn't he tell that she was burning? That she needed him?

Hearing his name stopped him. She felt him still next to her, then he rested his head against her chest and she felt his pulse beat in his temple. It was as quick as her own. When she tried to get him to move some more, he shook his head.

"I need a moment, just a moment to think," he whispered next to her skin.

She shook her head and closed her eyes. "No, let's not think. Not now." She pulled his head back until he looked up at her. "Please."

He closed his eyes and sighed. "You deserve more."

She felt as if he'd burned her with his words.

Then he looked at her and she could see that he was fighting a battle with himself. "God, I want you," he blurted out, "but not like this." He motioned around them.

For the first time in several minutes, she realized just how dirty they were. She laughed. She couldn't help it, the laughter just bubbled out.

"What's so funny?" he asked, stepping away from her.

"Everything," she blurted out.

Here she was, almost ready to have sex with a man she'd known less than a month, in what was no doubt one of the dirtiest places she'd ever been. And the fact was, she hadn't cared. She stopped laughing and looked over at him.

He was running his hands through his hair, causing some strands to stick straight up. There was a large spot of what looked like grease on his cheek and a slight layer of dirt all over him. She looked down at herself and frowned. She didn't look any better.

"I think I need a shower," she said. When he moaned, she glanced up at him. His eyes were closed, and his head had fallen backward.

"What?"

"Now I'm picturing you naked and wet," he said between his teeth. "I'm trying to be good here."

"Why?" She crossed her arms over her chest.

"Because you asked me to." He mimicked her pose. "Or don't you remember?"

She tilted her head and thought about it. She had told him she liked things the way they were. But seeing how sexy he looked staring at her, she couldn't stop herself from wanting him.

"A woman is entitled to change her mind." She smiled.

He shook his head. "You're tired and probably hungry." He sidestepped her when she reached out for him. She laughed, and he laughed with her.

"What do you say to grabbing some pizza?" He looked down at himself. "It's the only place in town where we won't be yelled at for being this dirty as we eat."

Since her stomach chose that moment to let out a loud growl, she nodded. "Sounds good."

By the time Marcus dropped her off at her apartment, she was back to her old self. As she stood in her little shower, trying not to dream of having hot water, she went over the reasons in her head why it was a bad idea for her to sleep with Marcus.

By the time she crawled onto her air mattress, she had thoroughly convinced herself that he'd done them both a favor.

After all, what did she really know about the man? She'd trusted someone like him before and look at what had happened to that relationship.

As she drifted off, her mind corrected her. No, Marcus was nothing like Tyler.

CHAPTER 10

There were only a few things in life that Marcus enjoyed more than sex. Demo was one of them. By the end of Tuesday night, every muscle in his body ached.

Shelly and he had knocked out one of the major walls that had needed to come down in her shop, but there had still been two others. Not to mention the heavy stonework that had covered the side wall and that would eventually be replaced with drywall. The stone was not only heavy, but a bitch to remove. It had taken four of them to get it all down and removed. By the end of the day, the entire demo had been completed. Now, the hard work could begin.

He sat in his living room and nursed a warm beer as he watched the game with his brother. He wished more than anything that he could be with Shelly instead.

That night he got little sleep and by the next morning, he was in a foul mood, which only escalated when he had to help unload all the wood from the delivery truck. To top it off, he'd banged his thumb and slammed his shins on the truck's lift.

By lunchtime, he was ready to call it a day. Not only were his men not cooperating, but now it appeared neither was the building. He'd scheduled Tom, one of his best electricians, and Joe, his best plumber, to be there first thing that morning.

Both men had shown up on time, but both men had run into issue after issue, which had slowed everything else down.

He'd hoped to have the new rooms framed out by the end of the day so ductwork, electric, and plumbing could be finished by the end of the month. But after all the problems they'd run into, they'd be lucky if everything got done by next year.

Tossing his hammer down, he stormed from what would end up being Shelly's office and marched out the front doors to cool off.

Sometimes a project just needed a little TLC. But with the lack of sleep and the sexual frustration building, he doubted he had any TLC to give it right now. At least not until he got a good night's sleep.

When he stepped out on the boardwalk into the light rain, he instantly felt better. He leaned against the railing and watched the waves crash against the sand.

This was his life. He loved working with his hands. Always had. He'd always used it as an escape from reality. Why was he now thinking of it as a distraction instead?

He turned around when he heard someone calling his name. Cassey was walking towards him, carrying a large bag under an even larger umbrella.

"Hey, I thought that was you." She smiled up at him.

"Taking a break?" she asked, trying to peek into the front windows. It wouldn't do her any good; they'd taped them off the day before, so people couldn't see in until it was ready.

"Yeah." He wiped his hand over his neck.

"Rough day?" She frowned a little at him.

He shrugged his shoulders. "Guess so."

"Anything I can help with?"

He looked down at her. Her long dark hair was tied back in two braids, reminding him of the scared little girl who had stepped out of Lilly's car and into his heart. He couldn't stop himself from smiling. "No." He shook his head as he tugged on the end of one of her braids. "I'm a big boy, I'll handle it."

She nodded and smiled. When she turned to go, she paused. "It doesn't have anything to do with Shelly, does it?"

He lied. "No."

"Good." She relaxed a little. "Because I really like her." Then Cassey turned and disappeared into the mist.

"Yeah, so do I," he said under his breath, realizing that was the real root of his problem.

Walking back into the building, he set aside his thoughts of Shelly and got back to work. After all of his men left, he stayed behind to finish up some of the work.

He didn't hear her walk in until she said his name behind him. He dropped his hammer and it landed on his foot.

"Oh!" She rushed forward, "Are you hurt?"

He chuckled. "No, I'm okay. Steel-toed boots." He nodded to his work boots.

"Oh." She frowned down at his foot.

"Is there something you wanted?" he asked, feeling a little frustrated that she was standing in front of him looking too damn sexy in black leggings with a low-cut green top that hugged every inch of her. Her hair was curled and flowing around her shoulders, making him wish he could bury his hands and face in it. He'd bet anything that it smelled like honey.

"No. Yes." She turned her eyes back to him. They'd been roaming over the space, taking in everything that had changed in the last two days. She shrugged her shoulders. "I just wanted to see…" She turned again and started walking around. "You've gotten so much done already."

He sighed as he realized he'd been watching her butt instead of listening to her. Forcing his eyes back to where her eyes would be, he tried to focus on keeping his wants in check.

"Actually, I feel like we're moving slower than normal. We had a few setbacks today."

"Oh?" She turned around and crossed her arms over her chest.

He nodded, his eyes glued to what the motion did to her breasts.

"Anything major?" she asked, taking a step towards him.

He shook his head no, his eyes still glued to her breasts. He knew it wasn't polite, but he wondered if she actually knew what she was doing? She had to, after all, coming down here dressed like that.

"Good." She sighed and turned back around. When she started to walk into the back room, he stopped her.

"Careful." He rushed over to take her arm. "There are still a lot of exposed nails in that room."

"Oh," she said under her breath. Then she blinked a few times and stepped back from him. "Listen, I wanted to talk to you about the other day."

He nodded and shoved his hands into his jean pockets. "Okay?"

"I…" She sighed. "I wanted to thank you. You know, for stopping." His heart deflated. "I mean, I'm not ready to jump back into a relationship so soon." She started pacing in front of him, waving her hands around as she spoke. "It's just that I'm not ready to fully be out on my own in that manner. I mean, so close after the fiasco last time."

He didn't understand half of what she was saying, but he listened to her and nodded when she looked at him. Finally, she turned to him with a slight smile.

"I hope you understand."

He nodded again but then started to shake his head no. "I'm sorry. What is it you're talking about?"

She let out a large sigh. "You know; I just don't want to get into another relationship so soon after breaking off my engagement."

That woke him up. He took a step back like he'd been hit over the head. "Engagement?"

Her chin dropped a little as she nodded her head. "I… I thought you knew. I mean…" She took a step closer. "After you found out who my father was, I assumed you knew about it. You know, piecing everything together."

He shook his head. "I know who your father is. I didn't say that I knew anything about you before."

"Oh." She groaned. "I've messed everything up." She started pacing again. Then she stopped and turned towards him abruptly. "I was engaged to one of my parents' friend's son. It was sort of an arranged thing between our folks. Well…" She looked down at her hands instead of his eyes. "I called it off when I moved here," she said quickly.

"You called it off, or you left him a voicemail like you did for your parents?"

Her eyes rushed to his and he saw the answer in them. Shaking his head, he reached down to pick up his hammer. "I guess it is a good thing I stopped the other night." He walked over and set his hammer into his toolbox.

"It wasn't like this," she said behind him. "I was never… I never…" He turned back to her. "I didn't feel that way towards Tyler. I mean, he didn't even propose to me. It was sort of just arranged."

He leaned back on the worktable. "It wasn't like what?"

She stopped looking at her hands and looked up at him.

My God, did he want everything spelled out? She let out a deep breath and blurted out, "Raw attraction."

He chuckled. "Is that what this is?" He crossed his arms over his chest and for a moment she forgot everything except the sight of the muscles in his arms, straining against the light material.

"I…" She shook her head. "I'm not sure." She locked onto his eyes again. "Can you label it yourself?"

He shook his head. "Fair enough. I guess I'm not sure what this is either."

She nodded once. "So…" She waited.

"So…" he said, smiling. "Engaged, huh?"

She closed her eyes and moaned. "Not anymore, I hope."

She heard his chuckle get closer and opened her eyes to see him coming towards her. "What do you say to having dinner with me?"

She smiled. "Sounds wonderful."

"Good. I can run home and shower then…"

"Why don't you just come upstairs? I've got pork chops in the oven already."

He frowned. "I'd like to shower first."

She smiled. "I've got a shower you can use if you insist."

He tilted his head. "I have a change of clothes in my truck. I'll grab them and be up in a minute."

She nodded and smiled, then surprised herself by putting her arms over his shoulders. "I meant what I said."

His hands went to her hips. "What?"

"That I'm very attracted to you." She leaned up and placed a hot kiss on his lips and then quickly turned and walked out. She could feel his eyes on her back as she swayed out.

By the time he knocked on her door, she felt completely in control of herself again. Seeing him sweaty did something to her. Maybe it was chemical? After all, she'd read an article somewhere that the odor of a sweaty man was highly attractive to women.

She tried to stay clear of him as he excused himself and disappeared into her bathroom. She'd been so busy avoiding him that she'd forgotten to mention the cold water.

She heard him gasp from the kitchen and tried not to chuckle. Maybe that would help speed along the water heater process.

By the time he stepped out of her bathroom, hair damp

and looking even sexier than before in a gray T-shirt and faded jeans, dinner was ready.

"Smells good." He set his bag down by the door and walked over to her. "Can I help with anything?"

She shook her head. "No, you've had a busy day working. Here." She handed him a beer and nodded to the table. "Go, sit down. I'll be just a moment more."

He smiled and took the beer. "A woman after my own heart." Sipping the beer, he walked over to the windows and looked out. The sky was dark since the clouds had yet to go away and it was still very foggy out.

Turning back to the food, she tossed the salad and pulled the pork chops from the oven.

"It's funny how many people stop and look at your sign. That was a really good idea." He took another sip of his beer.

She smiled, remembering how she'd used her paints to make a large sign that she had pasted in the front window, letting everyone who passed by know what was coming. "I had too much fun designing it. I can't wait until the big one is hanging over the door and the place is finished."

He nodded and then walked over to help her carry the plates of food to the small table.

"Speaking of finished things, I'll see about having your water heater installed this week."

She laughed. "Another reason I invited you to shower at my place."

He smiled. "Smart move. What was the first reason?"

Her lips twitched as she picked up her own beer and took a sip. The tangy taste did little to soothe her desires.

"So, I could picture you, how did you put it… naked and wet." She smiled and picked up her fork.

"You don't play fair." He frowned as he picked up his fork.

"I never promised to." She smiled and nibbled on her food. She was thrilled when his eyes heated, watching her lips as she enjoyed the meal.

By the time his plate was empty, she was sure he could see her excitement flow from her skin. They talked a little over the food, but for the most part, their eyes stayed locked as the heat level continued to rise.

When she stood to take the dishes to the sink, he shook his head and took her arm. "No, sit with me for a while longer."

She nodded and pulled her chair closer to him.

"You really need some furniture up here." He frowned looking around.

She chuckled. "Not until you're done with it. If I carry up anything now, we'll just have to haul it back down when construction starts."

He nodded. "Maybe we can move ahead on starting up here. I mean, there's no reason I can't have two teams going at once. I've got enough men. I have some guys finishing another project this Friday. I could have them start here on Monday morning."

"Really?" She bit her bottom lip. "I…" She looked around, "I'm not sure I'm ready."

He laughed. "Scared?"

She jutted her chin out. "Of course not."

His smile grew. "Good, then it's settled. The sooner you get a sofa; the sooner I could do this to you on it." He pulled her closer until she was practically sitting in his lap, and then he kissed her until she melted against him.

CHAPTER 11

The next few days, she woke to the sounds of construction below her. Each night, she and Marcus would have dinner together. They would either eat in her apartment or he would take her to someplace in town she hadn't been before.

Every night he would leave her breathless with his kisses and desperately wanting more. She was glad he wasn't pushing her and their relationship too fast, but part of her wished she had the nerve to jump him.

They spent that weekend getting her apartment ready for demo time. She repacked everything she owned and shoved it all along the brick wall. Even her air mattress would have to be deflated each day and rolled up.

"You might be without a shower for a while. If you want, you can stay at my place," he said as he set a heavy box of hers down.

The statement threw her off. "Stay at your place?"

"Sure." He bent down and picked up another box. "I

mean; it would be easier on you not being in the middle of all this." He looked around the almost empty room.

"What… what about Roman?"

He chuckled. "He'll be okay with you staying."

"I mean…" She bit her bottom lip. He stopped walking with the box and looked at her as his eyebrows shot up.

"Oh, God. I didn't mean…" His face turned a little pink. "I mean; I'd sleep on the sofa." He chuckled nervously.

She laughed a little. "I couldn't do that to you."

He smiled. "Trust me, I'd probably sleep a lot better knowing you were comfortable in the next room than I would if you were sleeping somewhere there wasn't running water and possibly even electricity."

"Really?" She looked around. "You think I'm not going to have power?" This did change things. She relied on the power to get her work done during the day while they were pounding away downstairs.

She still had inventory to purchase, display cases to order. She even had to price out some of the pieces she'd already bought and had in a storage unit just outside of town. Not to mention all the other vendor accounts she still had to secure.

Sighing loudly, she nodded. "I guess I could stay there during the worst parts of it. If it's okay with Roman."

He chuckled. "Trust me, Roman won't have an issue with sharing the apartment with a beautiful woman."

With Marcus's help, the weekend flew by and before she knew it, Monday morning was here, and the workers were knocking on her door.

At first, she stood around, not sure what to do, but then Marcus showed up and handed her a key to his apartment. "If you want, take your stuff over now. You can get some work done while we get this done." Then he smiled. "Trust me; you're only going to feel like you're in the way. Unless you want to put on your work clothes and…"

She shook her head no. "I have too much to do today." She frowned and bit her lower lip. Way too much.

When the men started working, she gathered up her stuff and headed to his apartment. She'd seen it briefly the day they'd gone over to get his tools. She parked her car and walked up to the door, knocking before she used the key he'd given her since she didn't know if Roman had left or not. She was thankful the place was dark.

Setting her stuff inside, she took a few minutes to look around. There were two bedrooms. One was so clean and organized she winced at how clean it was. The second room she immediately knew was Marcus's. It was clean, but nothing like Roman's room was. She relaxed a little. It wasn't that she didn't like cleanly people, just that both her parents and Tyler had been too organized. She had known too many people like that in her past.

Shaking some old memories off, she set up a workstation for herself at the dining room table and started making calls. By the time her stomach told her it was lunchtime, she had acquired two of the three new accounts she needed.

Her phone buzzed with a message and she was excited when a text from Marcus came through.

Heading over there with some lunch and my brother in tow.

She couldn't help it, she smiled. She really did like him and even though her head told her that she was on the verge of liking him too much, she pushed all of her fears aside.

When the two men arrived, she had already cleared all of her items off the table. She'd hung out with Roman several times at the bar and grill but hadn't really had an opportunity to talk to him.

By the time they'd finished eating lunch, she realized he was nothing like she'd imagined he would be. He was almost as funny as Marcus was. Even though he was dressed in business attire, she had the feeling he could roll up his sleeves and get dirty if the situation called for it.

"I occasionally work right alongside Marcus, but today I had a few meetings about the Spring Haven Home."

"Marcus has told me so much about your place. I'd love to see it for myself."

He smiled. "I can give you a tour later this week if you want."

"I can show her around," Marcus jumped in, wrapping his arm around her.

Roman laughed and said, "Message received." Then he winked at her and she couldn't help but smile.

After they left, she made a few more calls and placed a few more orders. Then she drove down and got a copy of her business license, which had finally been approved by the county. It was official. Shelly's was in business. She couldn't wait to get her space back and start getting the orders in.

When she drove up to the building, she was surprised to see the flurry of activity. Men were coming and going, carrying lumber in and wheelbarrows of trash out. She didn't want to disturb them but was curious how everything was going.

She could see by standing inside the front door that the back wall was up and the electrician was working on installing the overhead lights.

When she started heading up her stairs, she was met with a roadblock.

"No, you don't." Marcus smiled down at her. "Not yet. It's too crazy up there right now. Wait until my men leave." He took her hand and started walking back down the stairs.

She frowned a little but followed him back down.

"Here." He opened the front door for her. "I wanted to go over a few things in the back room with you."

When they walked into the back room, she was surprised that it was quiet and almost finished. Turning around, she took everything in.

She could just imagine her drawing table against the back wall, her sewing machine next to it, maybe a rack of clothes there, under the window.

"What do you see?" Marcus asked as he leaned against the door frame.

She smiled and then told him exactly what she planned for the room.

When she was done, he nodded and tilted his head as he looked around. "What about putting in one of those three-way mirrors right there? You know, so you could try on and check out the designs." He pointed to the corner. "You know like they have in dressing rooms?"

She nodded. "I'd planned to have one out front." She thought about it. "I suppose one back here would work too."

"Do you have a desk in mind for drawing?"

She shook her head no. "I was hoping to find a drawing table locally."

He smiled. "What if I built you something? I expect its kind of like a drafting table?" He looked at her and waited.

"Yes, but I wanted it a little larger, so it can double as a cutting table for the material."

He nodded and walked over to snatch a pencil and paper from his clipboard. The next two minutes he spent drawing something as she watched him.

His head was bent over the clipboard in complete focus. She took that time to admire how truly handsome he was. His dark eyelashes covered his blue eyes. He hadn't shaved that morning and the day's growth made him look a little dangerous and a whole lot sexier. She knew it would probably scratch her face, but she didn't think she'd mind the marks for the feeling of his lips on hers.

"Would something like this work?" He turned the paper around and showed her a table that could be used as a design table and as a flat surface to cut material on.

"Are those drawers?" She pointed to boxes along the top.

"Drawers or cubbies for pens, scissors, whatever." He shrugged his shoulders.

She would have never thought of it. Seeing the design, she instantly wanted it. Smiling, she nodded. "It's perfect."

He smiled at her. "We can build it in, right there." He walked over and took out a small tape measure from his pocket and started measuring.

"That's a perfect spot. I was thinking of having my sewing machine here." She motioned to the spot. "I have a table for it already that's about this big." She stepped off the size.

He nodded. "There would be enough room over here." He walked over and tilted his head. "Maybe for some hooks or…"

"What about a clothing rack?" She stood next to him.

"Yes." He took up his pencil again. "Like this." He turned it around.

She smiled at him. "Perfect."

About an hour later, they walked out of the back room to find that they'd been left alone. They could still hear workers moving upstairs, but the downstairs was empty.

"Looks like everyone's packing up for the day." He glanced down at his watch and nodded. "'Bout that time. We can head up in a few minutes."

She nodded and then walked around the larger room, dreaming of where everything would be.

"The dressing rooms are almost done," he said. She walked over and smiled at the two small rooms. "We will be hanging the doors soon, so it can all be painted." He smiled.

"I can't believe how fast everything is happening." She turned around in a circle.

He chuckled. "Now, if we could say the same about upstairs." He shook his head.

"Oh?" She turned towards him.

He nodded. "Had a few setbacks up there today. Demo didn't take long, except in the bathroom. Whoever put that tile up must have used cement to keep it there. It took four hours to knock it all out."

She desperately wanted to go look, but she could still hear men walking around up there.

"We can head up. I'm sure they're just cleaning up now."

She smiled and nodded.

Marcus watched Shelly walk around what used to be her apartment. There was a frown on her lips. He knew the place looked bad now and wanted to explain that it would get better.

He opened his mouth to speak, but she just shook her head at him. "I don't need explanation." She smiled. "I can tell that it's going to be great."

His smile was quick. "Good. Some people can't see the potential through the mess."

She chuckled. "I'm not one of those people. What about the bathroom?" She headed towards the back and he followed.

"It's gutted, and we finished knocking the wall down so we can enlarge it." He walked in and the space felt so much better than before.

"Look at how big it's going to be." She smiled at him. "Is the tub going here?" She stood in the spot.

"Yes, the glass shower will go here." He motioned to the spot.

"Sinks?" She pointed and when he nodded, she moved to where the old green toilet used to sit. "Toilet?" He nodded again. "It's going to be so much bigger than before." She walked towards the back and squealed. "Oh, look at my closet." She spun in the space.

He followed and laughed. "I can never get over how women respond to a large walk-in closet."

She laughed and rushed over to hug him. He laughed with her and started spinning her around. Then he couldn't stop himself from kissing her. The way she responded to him had his hand shaking on her hips as he pulled her closer.

When they finally moved apart, he smiled, noticing that they were both a little breathless.

"I... I guess we can't deny what's between us," she said with her eyes glued to his lips. His eyes went to hers in response.

He shook his head no. "Why are we even trying?"

She stepped back and took a deep breath. She shoved her hands into her pockets and shrugged her shoulders. "I guess there's no real reason." She looked up at him again. "I... I don't think I'm ready for anything too serious at the moment. Not after Tyler..."

He walked over to her and took her shoulders until she looked up at him. "Why don't we just continue to take things slow, like we've been. You know, see how it goes." He was relieved when she smiled and nodded. "Good, now what do you say to some dinner?"

She smiled and nodded. "Sounds great."

"Good. I think I need a shower first." He looked down at himself and frowned.

"Don't forget you need a shave, too." She reached up and brushed her hand over his stubbly chin.

An hour later, they walked out of his apartment together. He'd showered and changed into some of his best clothes, and she'd changed into a simple black dress that hugged her curves. She'd finished the dress off with a brightly colored scarf around her shoulders. He'd tried to convince her to carry a jacket with her instead, but she'd just shaken her head and smiled.

"There is a cost for looking good." She laughed at his

frown. He had to admit, she did look good. Especially when he watched her walk towards him in three-inch heels.

He drove them to Sea Side, a small town about half an hour away. Here, prices were higher due to the large number of tourists that flooded the picturesque town year-round.

He parked his truck and helped her down, enjoying the feeling of her in his arms. Then they walked along the sidewalk until he pulled her into Marina's, one of the best Italian restaurants along the coast and one of the most romantic places to eat. They sat at a small table along the large glass wall that overlooked the beach below them. They had almost an hour before sunset.

He ordered a bottle of wine as they waited for their food to be delivered.

"I just can't get over the view." She sighed and rested her chin on her hands. "Does it ever get old for you?" She glanced at him.

He shook his head, not seeing the beauty outside his window, but glued to the one sitting across from him. No, he doubted it would ever get old sitting across from her. She smiled, and he thought for sure she could read his thoughts.

She couldn't stop glancing at Marcus as they ate. Even the sun setting over the water outside held little interest for her.

"How's the food?" he asked softly.

She nodded. "Good." But truth be told, she'd barely registered the taste. Her mouth watered at the thought of him close to her, kissing her again.

He brushed her hand with his across the table. She decided to be a little brazen since she'd made up her mind about him and reached out with her foot to rub his leg with her toes. She watched his eyes heat, then he asked for their check and quickly put down enough cash to cover the cost.

"Let's get out of here," he said in a low voice. All she could do was nod her head and keep up with him as he pulled her through the crowded room.

When they reached his truck, he pulled her close to him as his mouth covered hers. Her back was up against his truck as his hands roamed over her hips.

When he pulled back, he smiled. "Roman's staying in Spring Haven tonight. We have the place all to ourselves."

She felt her breath hitch as she smiled and nodded back. She reached for the door handle and he helped her up into his truck. They rode in silence for a while, until finally, he chuckled.

"I feel like a teenager getting ready to sneak a girl into the house while my folks are out."

She laughed. "I've never snuck into a boy's house before."

"No?" He glanced at her. She shook her head.

"Ever sneak a guy into your place?"

She chuckled. "Never. My parents were like hawks. I couldn't even sneak to the kitchen for a snack without them knowing."

He shook his head. "Kids, teenagers"—he glanced at her— "are supposed to sneak behind their folks back."

"Oh?" She watched him nod. "Is that what you're going to say when your teenager sneaks a boy into her room?"

He frowned. "Hell no." He looked over at her. "Good point."

"Of course, if you had a son, you'd sing a different tune."

He smiled. "Of course. It's just different."

She shook her head. "Men."

He chuckled.

When he parked down the street from his place, he sighed. "Damn," he said under his breath.

"What?"

"One brother cooperated, the other I'm about to kill."

CHAPTER 12

He nodded towards a Jeep parked a few feet away. "Cole?" she asked. Marcus nodded.

"He stays here when he's in town."

"I thought he was in Africa."

"Yeah, so did everyone else. What I wouldn't give to have your place finished."

She chuckled and moved closer to him, running her hands in his hair. "There's always time."

He nodded and closed his eyes on a groan. "Yeah, I suppose."

She used that moment to place her lips on his. When his hands ran over her, she moaned and desperately wished for some more alone time.

His hands moved up her skirt and she felt his callused fingers rub gently over her legs. She moaned and moved so he could run them higher. Her fingers were in his hair as she kept his mouth against hers. When his finger moved beneath her panties, she jerked in his hands and cried out.

She heard him moan as his finger ran over the slickness of her, then again when he dipped it deep into her. She bucked her hips towards him and dug her nails into his shoulders as he pleased her.

"More…" he said as he pushed her skirt up higher with his other hand. "I've got to have…" He moved down as she leaned back against the door. "Mmmm," he moaned as his mouth touched her inner thigh. Her fingers went to his hair as he ran his mouth over every inch of her.

"Marcus…" she cried out as she felt herself exploding.

When he moved closer to her, he sighed and whispered. "Damn, this isn't how I imagined…" He rested his forehead against hers.

She chuckled. "You did mention acting like teenagers. What says that more than doing this in a parked car?"

He chuckled. "I suppose you're right." Then he looked down at her. "Don't lock your door tonight."

She shook her head no and swallowed deeply. The heat that was in his eyes told her that he'd break down her door if he had to.

When they reparked and walked into the apartment, Cole was on the sofa watching a game.

"There you guys are." He smiled.

"Thought you were in Africa, trying to drown yourself?" Marcus said, walking into the kitchen to grab a beer.

"Naw, been there done that." Then he smiled at her. "Hey, come sit down, you're just in time for the second quarter."

She glanced over at Marcus, who just shrugged his shoulders and held up a beer in question. She nodded and sat next to his brother.

"Date night?" He glanced at her as she toed off her heels.

She nodded and took the beer from Marcus, who sat next to her and put his arm over her shoulder.

"Well, don't you two clean up nicely." Cole smiled.

"Where's Trilla?" Shelly leaned back against Marcus's chest and enjoyed the feeling of being so close to him.

Cole shrugged his shoulders. "I think she's back in Europe." He took a drink of his own beer.

"My brother never hangs onto a woman long. I think it's his winning personality," Marcus said sarcastically as he ran a hand over Shelly's hair.

"At least I have women." Cole winced as he glanced towards Shelly. "Sorry, that usually works, but now that he's got you…" He took another drink of his beer then set it down quickly. "This beer is warm." He glanced at the fridge and frowned. "Well, since I know that you just grabbed the last two beers in the fridge, I'm going down to Cassey's for a cold one and to watch the game on the big screen." He stood up and walked to the door. "Don't wait up for me." He winked at Shelly and left.

"Smart man," Marcus said next to her ear before he started nibbling on it, causing goosebumps to raise all over her skin. "Want to do some more teenage stuff here on the sofa with me?" he asked as he moved closer to her. She scooted down with him until he hovered over her, a smile on her lips.

"Mmm, I think I can think of a few things we can do."

He ran his hands up her legs and she tugged on his shirt. When finally, he pulled away and pushed it off his shoulders, she sighed as she ran her hands over his muscles. She'd always dreamed of running her hands over someone like him. His skin was still tan from last summer. Her hands looked so small and white against his skin.

Then he was kissing her again as he tugged on the neckline of her dress. His mouth ran over her shoulder blade then further down as more skin was exposed. She arched into him, wanting more.

"You're so soft and you taste like honey," he said between raining kisses over her skin.

Her nails dug into his skin and when she leaned up to trail her mouth over his chest, he tensed a little. Then he was removing her clothing, and she desperately wanted to feel him next to her skin.

"Shelly…" he said against her breast. Then he took her

nipple into his mouth and sucked until she arched into him on a moan.

She wrapped her legs around his hips and felt his erection against her. Wanting more, she reached for his jeans only to have him pull away.

He shook his head and then quickly stood up, picking her up in his arms. She smiled and placed kisses along his collarbone as he walked them back to his room.

When he set her down gently on his bed, he stood and looked down at her. His eyes were full of desire as he ran them over every inch of her. For her part, she was doing the same. His shirt was gone and she could see just how impressive he really was. She wondered why she'd put off being with him when she felt this close to him. She tried to hold off on the emotions and just think about the now, but when he was looking at her with those blue eyes filled with more than just desire, she had a hard time with it.

"I love looking at you." He smiled and reached to help her remove her tight dress.

After wiggling out of the silky material, she knelt before him on the edge of his bed as he ran his eyes over her.

Marcus looked at Shelly as she knelt before him in nothing but a skimpy pair of black panties and a matching bra. Her skin looked like silk, and he knew it would taste like warm honey. Her hair was tangled from his hands as it fell around her shoulders.

When she reached up for him, he stepped closer to her, toeing off his shoes before he moved to her on the bed.

She immediately reached for his jeans again and he couldn't stop the smile. "In a hurry?"

She smiled and nodded. "I like speed," she said, pulling him closer for a kiss. He dodged her mouth and chuckled.

"I like to take it slow. To savor everything." He ran the back of his fingers down her shoulder and watched her eyes fall shut. "I love to touch everything, taste everywhere." He dipped his head to her other shoulder and ran his mouth over the curve that he found there. "It makes me wild feeling your skin heat under my hands."

She moaned and he watched her hands go limp next to her. He couldn't stop the smile, knowing that he was slowly driving her crazy like she'd been doing to him for days.

He spread his hand on her lower back and nudged her down until she lay beneath him. Using his knees, he spread her legs wider until he could rest between them, his erection pushing against his jeans and against her silk panties. He felt her twitch with movement, then her hips started to move slowly, and he closed his eyes on a moan as she rubbed his cock slowly. When her legs once again wrapped around his hips, he tried to remind himself that he had wanted to go slow, wanted to enjoy every minute of being with her.

Her mouth started moving over his skin as her hands went to his jeans again and pushed them down. This time he didn't argue. When he sprang free, her hand was there to catch him, to hold him gently as she started to stroke, slowly then faster.

His hips started to thrust towards her as his hands went over her panties, then he was pulling them aside and pushing his fingers into her heat. She was warm and wet, perfect for him.

Their mouths met again as they continued to please one another. He enjoyed the little noises she made as he stroked her. When he felt her come for him, he slowly pulled back and tossed his jeans on the floor next to his bed and then yanked a package of condoms from his night-stand and moved back to her.

She was watching him, her hair fanned out on his bed, a smile on her lips. Her hands reached out for him. When he came back to her, she grabbed his head and placed kisses along his neck as he sheathed himself for her.

Using his hands to move her hips up, he positioned himself outside of her. As he slid into her, she moaned and threw her head back. Her fingers dug into his hips as he held still, trying not to explode too quickly with his desire.

She was everything he'd dreamed she would be. Her skin glowed as he took her, and her eyes warmed to a rich honey color. He could spend the rest of his life watching her come for him.

This time when he felt her convulse around him, he followed her into the bliss.

She felt his breath on her neck and smiled. Their skin had cooled enough that she realized there was quite a chill in the room. She started to shiver a little.

"Cold?" he asked against her skin.

She sighed. "Not really. I guess my skin is just cooling off." She giggled.

He leaned up and smiled down at her. "We could

always heat things up again." He leaned down and kissed her lips, causing her skin to boil again.

She'd never experienced anything like this before with anyone. Of course, she'd only been with a few men—okay, two—before Marcus. But that didn't stop her from knowing that this was different. Special.

She kissed him back with everything she had. When his hips started moving against hers, she wrapped her legs around his and held on one more time.

Looking up into his blue eyes, she couldn't stop herself from feeling everything. So much that it almost hurt. Closing her eyes, she tried to deny that she was starting to care for him more and more. She'd always been cautious of getting too close.

But her new life wouldn't take the same turn it had in the past. Not if she worked at it and believed things were different.

His hand slowly ran up her leg, then he moved her until her knee was close to her chest. She lost her breath at the feeling of him inside her, filling her completely.

"Come for me," he whispered next to her skin. "Don't hold out." When he kissed her, she was unable to deny him anything.

CHAPTER 13

Sometime in the night, he must have covered them with his blankets. He always got too hot, even in winter. Kicking them off his legs, he snuggled closer to Shelly and smiled when he buried his face in her hair. She smelled so wonderful.

He could definitely get used to having her in his bed. She moved a little, tangling her legs with his, and the silky softness of them almost undid him.

He loved women. All different kinds of them. But he especially loved the silky soft kind. The kind that smelled and tasted like honey.

He drifted off again as sweet dreams of the two of them filled his head.

When he woke, he was alone in the bed. Instantly he felt loss, but then he heard his shower running and smiled.

When he pulled back the shower curtain, she gasped and tried to cover herself.

"Little late for that, don't you think?" He chuckled and

stepped in behind her, wincing at how hot the water was. His hands went to her hips and pulled her close.

"You scared me," she said, pushing her hair out of her eyes.

He chuckled. "Sorry. Up a little early today, aren't you?" He ran his mouth over her neck, enjoying himself.

She leaned a little, giving him more access to her neck. "Mmm." She leaned back into him. "I have to drive into Panama City today for a meeting with a supplier."

He ran his hands up the front of her slowly. "Hmmm," he said against her skin. "What time do you need to be there?"

"Nine." She sighed and turned around and wrapped her arms around his shoulders. "That gives us just enough time to enjoy this shower." She smiled and kissed him.

"Good." He pushed her up against the shower wall, and his hands roamed over every inch of her. When he slid into her, twin moans of delight filled the bathroom.

Slick skin against slick skin. Water ran down both of them as he tried to keep his footing in the shower. Her nails dug into his arms as he braced himself against the wall, holding them both upright. One of her legs was wrapped around his hips as he became more and more out of control.

Finally, he felt her tighten around him, and he let go himself a few seconds later.

"I can't believe we didn't kill ourselves." She chuckled against his shoulder.

"Maybe we weren't trying as hard as we should have." He leaned back and smiled at her. The hot water hit him right between the shoulder blades. "We've got to do something about this heat." He bent down and turned the heat down.

She whined a little. "After three weeks of having only cold water, I was really enjoying that." She moved around him and stood in the spray. "I was starting to feel like I was boiling myself." She looked down. He noticed that her pale skin did look a little red.

"Take as many hot showers as you want." He smiled and dumped some shampoo into his hands to lather himself. Then he ran his soapy hands down her as well.

"Mmm, that feels so good." She leaned into his hands. "I may never want to leave your shower." She giggled.

Just then, they heard his brother calling out.

"Hey, I'm back. Hope everyone's decent," Cole called out. Marcus chuckled as Shelly gasped and tensed.

"He won't come in here." He frowned down at her and watched her cheeks turn a rosy color.

"I… I'd better get ready. I don't want to be late." She ducked under the spray to rinse off and then stepped out.

After showering, he dressed and headed out to throw together some breakfast. He knew Cole wouldn't wait long and would probably eat everything in the fridge. He wanted to make sure he could sit down with Shelly before she left for the day.

By the time he was done making scrambled eggs and toast, she was stepping out of his room looking damn sexy in a cream skirt and teal blouse. Her hair was piled up on top of her head and several strands of hair fell around her face. Her lips looked very inviting painted a rosy pink.

"You clean up pretty nicely," Cole said just before he shoveled some of the eggs into his mouth.

She smiled. "Thank you." She walked over and took

the cup of coffee he was holding out for her. Before she could snatch it away, he leaned in and kissed her solidly on the lips, just to make sure his brother knew where they stood.

"I have some breakfast for you before you head out."

She frowned a little, then took the cup and sat down by the plate he'd set down.

"Damn, Marcus. I don't know how you do it, but you make the best eggs," Cole said with his mouth half full. "Bet you didn't know that he cooks too." Cole smiled at Shelly.

Marcus thought he saw Shelly's cheeks turn a little redder, as she shook her head no.

"Talented." He shook his head. "Except when it comes to surfing." Cole laughed.

"Don't you have somewhere to be?" Marcus warned.

"Hmm?" Cole looked up at him. "Oh, no. Not until later." He dismissed his brother. Marcus was sure he'd received his warning, but he went on ahead and told the embarrassing story of how Marcus had broken his arm, anyway.

By the time Shelly was done with her breakfast, she was laughing so hard, he was sure his manly reputation was tarnished.

"Well..." She stood up with her plate. "I'd better be going if I'm going to make my meeting in time." She set her plate in the sink then turned to him. "I'll see you later tonight." She walked over and kissed his cheek. He felt pretty special until she did the same to his brother, who immediately puffed up his chest and winked at him.

Marcus frowned as he followed her outside.

"What do you say to hitting Cassey's tonight for

dinner?" He pulled her to a stop by placing his hand on her shoulder.

She smiled and nodded. "Sounds wonderful. I shouldn't be too late." She got in her car and he watched her drive away.

When he walked back into the apartment, Cole was sitting on the couch watching the news.

"Thinking about hanging onto this one?" he asked without looking at him.

"If you don't have anything better to do today, put on some work clothes. We could use your help down at Shelly's." He walked out of the room to grab the rest of his stuff.

Cole and Roman ended up helping for the entire day. It was nice having two extra hands around. By the time his men called it quits, he was sure they had just jumped the schedule ahead by a whole day.

When they got back to the apartment, he frowned when Shelly's car wasn't parked out front. Showering, he changed and sat with his brothers and watched some high-lights of last night's game as he waited for Shelly to return.

Shelly was running late. Her meeting had gone exception-ally well. There were just too many items to choose from at this supplier. She couldn't wait to have her space filled with all the wonderful things.

She hadn't ever been to Panama City and decided to spend some time looking around. She even drove to the beach since it was a rather warm day out.

It was hard to explain, but she felt absolutely

wonderful and wanted to enjoy her time as much as she could. When she finally looked down at her watch, she realized she was running a little later than she'd planned for. Pulling out her phone, she texted Marcus that she would meet him at Cassey's since she'd lost track of time.

He responded back almost immediately.

Hope you had a good meeting and day.

The best. Panama City is very nice. The meeting went wonderfully. Tell you more over food. I'm starved.

Good, see you there. I missed you today.

She felt her heart flutter a little as she started to drive out of town. It was so nice not to be questioned about every little detail, where she was and what she'd been doing. It wasn't as if she'd had a leash on, but she might as well have, the way she grew up.

Freedom was something she'd never really experienced, and now that she'd had a taste of it, she planned to do everything in her power to keep it. The drive back to Surf Breeze was wonderful. She couldn't believe how many deer came out at dusk and ate alongside the road. She'd lost count at twenty-three. When she drove into town, she sighed.

She'd never really felt at home anywhere before. Even though she'd only been here a little over a month now, she really did feel like this was her home.

Pulling into her parking spot, she desperately wished she had time to run over and see all that they had accomplished during the day, but she knew Marcus would be waiting for her.

She couldn't help but smile when she walked into the Boardwalk Bar and Grill and saw Marcus surrounded by his family, looking happy as the entire group laughed at something he'd said. When his eyes zeroed in on her, he shrugged his shoulders and stood up and started walking over to her.

"Sorry." He nodded to his family. "They just won't take a hint about not tagging along."

She smiled. "It's okay, I like the company." She reached up and kissed him right in front of everyone. She thought she heard a cheer that was cut off short. When she looked, Roman was rubbing his stomach and Cassey, who was sitting right next to him, was frowning over at him.

"They may be nosy, but they mean well," Marcus whispered before they walked over and joined the group.

She'd never had the pleasure of having family meals before. No big holiday get-togethers with aunts or uncles and cousins. She'd never experienced anything like what she was experiencing with his family now for the second time in just under a month.

She laughed and joked with them, this time feeling a little more comfortable than she had the first time around. Marcus had suggested the Red Snapper Po Boy, which had ended up being the best sandwich she'd ever had. She'd taken Cassey's suggestion of a drink, a frozen Pineapple Sunset, one of the bar's signature specialty drinks. It had been as delicious as it was beautiful.

By the time Marcus tugged on her hand to get her to move from the seat, her head was feeling a little numb from the drink. She felt wonderful.

"I'm going to go show Shelly what we accomplished today. I'm sure she's dying to see it all."

She nodded. "It's so wonderful seeing it come together." She sighed as everyone smiled at them. "Good night, everyone."

"You'll be happy and surprised at how much got done today. Roman and Cole lent a hand."

"Oh?" She wrapped her arm in his as they walked along the boardwalk. The beach was too dark for her to see the water, but she could still hear the waves lightly lapping up on the sand. Even that sound made her think of home.

"Did I mention that I put an offer on the place on Sugar Sand Lane?"

"And?" She turned a little towards him.

"Haven't heard back from them yet. Apparently, the owners are out of state. That's one of the reasons the place is in such need of repair."

"Well, I know you'll get it. Just don't start work on it until my place is done." She smiled.

He laughed. "No. I'll be working on it on my own time."

"Oh? I thought you were going to fix it up and sell it?"

He shook his head and pulled her to a stop just outside her door. "No, this one's personal. I'm getting tired of sharing a place with my brothers. Besides, I need some room to grow, and to enjoy."

She smiled up at him, knowing exactly what he meant. Even though she hadn't been escaping brothers, she had been escaping family by moving here.

"Here now." He took hold of her shoulders and turned her towards the doors. "Close your eyes." She did as he asked and trusted him to lead her inside without bumping her into anything.

"Okay," he said, nudging her into position. "Open."

When she did, she gasped. She had a workspace. Not only that, but her workstation desk was completed.

"It still needs to be sanded and stained," he said from behind her somewhere.

She shook her head as she took in everything. The small cubbies, the smooth area that she'd use to sketch or plan out her material. Everything was perfect.

"It's wonderful. Perfect." She turned to him, a huge smile on her face. She watched the worry in his eyes disappear after hearing her words. Then she wrapped her arms around his shoulders and kissed him solidly.

She enjoyed him for a moment and then pulled away. "I want a better look." She laughed, knowing that she could get lost in him if she didn't step away now.

She ran her fingers over the smooth wood. It could use a fine sanding and paint, something she was itching to do herself. She liked the height of the desk area. There were even cubbies the right size to hold rolled up material and patterns and smaller ones for pens or scissors. It really was perfect.

"I can't believe you finished this in one day." She turned to him.

He was watching her, smiling. "I wouldn't have been able to if it wasn't for my brothers helping out."

She nodded. "Then I owe them one." She turned back to it.

"Don't you want to see what the men accomplished upstairs?"

She turned quickly and nodded. "I'm dying to."

He took her hand and they walked up the stairs. "They have the closet area completed and ready for paint. Your bathroom..." He shook his head. "They ran into some plumbing issues, but I'm told it will all be fixed by Friday.

The guy had some issues installing your tankless water heater, or so I was told."

He stood back and opened her door. The walls up here were prepped and ready for paint as well. The room felt huge, even though they had added two new walls dividing the space off in the back for a bedroom. Her kitchen area was looking better. She could see large boxes and when she walked over, he followed.

"Your cabinets arrived today. Want to take a look?"

She nodded and started tugging on the box. He laughed. "Here, let me." She stood back as he pulled out a pocketknife and cut the top of one of the boxes open.

She helped him yank the cardboard open and smiled when she saw the rich cream-colored French cabinets. "Oh, I can't wait to see them in place."

"We'll start hanging them in a few days after the electrician is done with the wiring and the drywall is finished." He nodded to the mess of wires hanging out of the walls. "Plus the plumbing. Once that's all done, these will go in, and we can start painting and working on the flooring."

"It's all happening so fast." She smiled. "I can't thank you enough."

He laughed. "The longer we take; the more money it costs you. Downstairs should be one hundred percent by this time next month." He frowned a little. "Up here, shortly after."

She could tell why he'd turned sad. She had enjoyed last night and if she had to be honest with herself, she was hoping they'd have more nights like it in the future.

She walked over to him. "It'll be nice showering without worrying if your brother will walk in on us." She watched him smile.

"I…" He shook his head. "Are you sure you won't mind me sticking around here?"

She nodded. "I kind of like having you around."

"Good." He dipped his head lower and kissed her, and she wished the place was already done and that they had a large bed to fall back on together.

CHAPTER 14

It took two days to finally hear a counteroffer for the place on Sugar Sand Lane, which he immediately accepted.

Shelly had spent those two days sanding and painting her new work area. She also had a few old display cases that she'd made look brand new with a coat of paint. He was glad to see her take such care when she worked.

When he got off the phone with Susan, he immediately went downstairs to tell Shelly the good news, but she was on the phone and looked like she had been crying. Closing the new door to her office area behind him, he waited until she was off the phone.

"Problem?" he asked, causing her to jump a little. He'd thought she'd heard him enter, but realized she'd been too engrossed in the phone conversation to hear.

"Oh…" She turned and looked down at the paint on her hands. "No, just the same old stuff." She sighed.

"Your folks?" He walked closer to her as she nodded. "They still expect you to come home?"

She nodded again. "It's like I'm talking to a brick wall." She sat down quickly on her work chair. "They just don't believe that I'm down here to stay."

"You are," he said and winced when it came out sounding more like a question. She glanced at him and nodded.

"Of course, I am. I'm home." She closed her eyes and sighed again. "For the first time in my life, I feel like I'm where I'm supposed to be." She looked at him and he could see the weariness and determination in her eyes.

He walked over and knelt down in front of her. "They'll come around, sooner or later. Just be strong." He took her hand in his, noticing the paint splatters on her fingers.

"I doubt it, but..." She tried to smile. "I hope so."

He stood and pulled her with him. "This is looking good." He nodded to her work area. "I had to admit, I had my doubts when you told me you were going to paint it instead of staining it, but it looks wonderful."

She nodded. "The cream color matches the cabinets that will go there." She nodded to the spot overhead. The two hanging cabinets were still in boxes along the outer wall. He had plans to hang them the following day.

"We'll start painting the walls in here in a few days." He smiled at her.

"I can't wait to see it all done. I have my first shipment of products coming in less than two weeks." She sighed. "Two weeks." He watched worry cross her eyes. Then he remembered why he'd come down here.

"It's official. I bought the house on Sugar Sand Lane."

She turned to him, her eyes going wide. "They took your offer?"

He laughed and shook his head. "I took their counteroffer."

She launched herself at him and he spun her around while she laughed and congratulated him.

"This calls for a celebration. How about I take you out tonight?" she said. He was happy to watch the sadness leave her eyes.

He chuckled. "Okay, or we could order pizza and stay in." He tightened his arms around her. "Roman is staying at Dad's tonight and Cole left earlier this morning to head to Hawaii again. We have the place all to ourselves."

She smiled. "Sounds like a good plan." When she kissed him, he couldn't stop his heart from skipping. Would it always be this way with her? He desperately wished so.

As time went by and they got closer to completing her place, she became very busy. He tried to help her out with some of the paperwork she had piled up but ended up only getting in her way.

"What you need is an employee," he said one evening when she'd sat at her computer, stressing about her orders.

"I can't afford one until my doors are closer to being open." She sighed. "Actually, I had planned on hiring a few people."

"You'd better start looking now. You have less than two weeks before we'll be done."

"What? That can't be right." She pulled out her phone and frowned down at the screen. "It's the fifteenth. How can it be the fifteenth already?"

He walked over to her. "Speaking of forgetting things. I wanted to invite you to dinner with my family. You know, in Spring Haven. My dad and Julie have been asking about you. They wanted a chance to have you over again." He'd meant to ask her days ago, but every time he opened his mouth, he felt nervous. He'd never invited a woman to his house for an official dinner with his family before.

"I…" She nodded slowly and closed her mouth to swallow. "I'd love to have dinner with you and your family."

Then his mind cleared. "The phone call… You haven't changed your mind, have you?" He frowned.

"What?" She looked at him.

"I know your family must miss you terribly. I hope you haven't changed your mind about going back."

She shook her head and then started laughing. "Oh, if that was only the case. I doubt my parents miss having me in the state." He shook his head, not sure what to say. She dropped her arms and took a few steps away from him. "No, they can't persuade me to go back with just a phone call." He heard the hurt in her voice. She began rubbing her forehead, so he walked over and started massaging her shoulders lightly. "What my mother wanted was for me to get back *home* so I could attend my engagement party next weekend." She chuckled.

"You're having an engagement party next weekend?" His hands dropped to his sides.

She laughed again and closed her eyes. "Nooo, my mother is having an engagement party for me next weekend. I officially broke off my engagement last month."

He felt the blood rush back to his body in relief.

She turned away from him and walked over to the small window that overlooked the back alley. He could tell she wasn't really seeing anything but was deep in her own thoughts. He walked up behind her again and wrapped his arms around her.

"I'm sorry," he whispered in her hair and placed a soft kiss on the top of her head.

She shook her head. "Your family has been so wonderful." She turned in his arms. "You've been so wonderful. You have nothing to be sorry for." She smiled up at him.

He didn't know what to say. At that moment, no quick-witted remarks came to him. He swallowed and felt the lump in his throat grow. Closing his eyes, he rested his forehead on hers.

"Take me home so I can have some cold pizza and beer to celebrate you becoming a homeowner." She pulled back and he noticed a slight smile on her lips. Bending down, he kissed them and nodded.

The next few days were filled with work. Every muscle in her body ached as she helped Marcus and his men complete the finishing touches on the shop area. She helped with painting, although the man who came with a spray machine did most of the work, and all that was needed by hand was some of the trim and touch up.

It took a full day to hang the sign above the outer doors, and by that evening, *Shelly's* was lit up in cool neon teal for everyone to see, with *Boutique* in white, underneath it.

The flooring was delivered and was scheduled to be installed the next morning, which was just in time because she'd had boxes of product arrive early. She'd stored them in the back room, still unopened, but she itched to dig into them and look at everything.

Wendy had come by on her day off and helped as much as she could. It was nice having another woman around.

"I can't wait to shop here," Wendy said, sitting back on her heels. They were both kneeling in the back room trying to finish painting the baseboards around all the boxes that had been delivered. "Are you sure we can't open just one box?" Wendy tapped the largest one with a smile.

Shelly laughed. "Maybe after we finish and get cleaned up."

"Woohoo!" Wendy was way more motivated after that, and the rest of the painting had gone very quickly.

In the end, they opened all of the boxes and looked through everything. She could still hear the men moving around up in her apartment and knew that Marcus was going to give her a ride home that night since they'd ridden together that morning.

"So," Wendy said as she held up a sundress in front of her. "You and Marcus?"

Shelly smiled. "Yeah." She nodded her head. "It just kind of snuck up on me."

"What did?" Wendy asked, setting the dress down and picking up another one.

"He did." Shelly shook her head and laughed a little.

"Oh please, you'd have to be blind or dead not to enjoy a Grayton man. Every one of them is good looking." Wendy sighed. "Of course, some of them I just want to murder." She laughed.

"So, what's between you and Cole?" Shelly asked after the laughter died down.

Wendy put down the dress and looked at her with a slight frown on her lips. "The man infuriates me. I mean, just to see how reckless he is with his life." She put her hands on her hips. "Not to mention all the women he parades around with. It's like he has no regard for their feelings. Does he even know that he's a womanizer?" She shook her head and Shelly could see the anger growing there. Instantly she wanted to change the subject. Looking around she saw her chance.

"Here, this box next…" She opened the larger box. "Shoes." That did it. Wendy rushed over and for the next twenty minutes, they tried on every last pair.

When Marcus walked in, they decided on dinner at the bar and grill. It was easier than trying to cook for all four of them, especially since Cassey and Luke might join in. It was a habit that she was beginning to really enjoy. Since it was Wendy's night off, she joined them in the large booth near the back.

Shelly noticed that Cole maneuvered it so he sat right beside Wendy. By the end of the dinner, she'd realized that Cole actually enjoyed riling Wendy up. He would purposely say things that everyone at the table knew would provoke Wendy. She'd even seen Marcus and Roman exchange looks multiple times.

It was actually quite funny to watch the scene. Even though she could see Wendy getting frustrated, she could also see that it was a game that the two of them had been playing for some time.

After everyone went their separate ways, Marcus took her hand and they walked along the boardwalk for a while. When he stopped outside her store, he leaned back on the railing and just looked at the building. She couldn't help herself, she felt her heart race just thinking about opening day.

"It's looking wonderful, isn't it?" She sighed and leaned back against his shoulder.

He nodded and looked down at her. "We'll be done by next weekend. When's opening day?"

She frowned a little, trying to calculate. "I'll have to get the computer set up and input all the stock. Not to mention tag everything and…" She dropped off. There was too much to list. Shutting her eyes, she sighed. "I'll probably need a month to get ready."

He chuckled. "Hire a couple employees. It'll take you half the time."

She looked up at him. He was right. It was time she hired some help. "I'll put a sign in the window first thing tomorrow."

He nodded. "The flooring should be done in two days."

"That quick?" She turned and wrapped her arms around him and loved the feeling of him pulling her closer.

He nodded. "Phillip and his gang are good and fast. They might even have it done sooner."

She smiled. "I don't know what I would have done without you." She leaned up and placed a kiss on his lips.

"I think the same." He cupped her face and took the kiss deeper. By the time he pulled away, she was a little breathless and was wishing her apartment upstairs was completed.

Just then her phone rang and she chuckled nervously as she pulled it out of her pocket. When she saw her mother's number on the display, her heart dropped. Stepping away from Marcus, she answered it.

"Hello, Mother."

"Shelly, I hope you're happy. This is really childish of you, you know. After all, that your father and I have done for you." She heard her mother sigh. "Not to mention how you left poor Tyler. And to think that his family is still willing to forgive you. We've moved your party to next month. You have one week to get back here and make your apologies to us and to the Daltons. Not to mention all of your friends."

Shelly started rubbing her forehead. "I've told you Mother; I'm not coming back. I have a new life here—"

"You have a life here," her mother cut in.

"I stopped living there. I'm no longer tied into anything in DC."

"Really?" Her mother sounded hurt. Shelly knew it was her game and she'd stepped into the next move blindly. "I suppose you're no longer tied to your father and me? Well, really!"

"That's not what I meant, Mother, and you know it. I meant…" She sighed as Marcus's arms came around her.

"It's one thing to leave school early, but it's a totally different thing to leave Tyler at the altar."

"I didn't leave him at the altar. There was no official date set for the wedding." She leaned back as Marcus started rubbing the tension from her shoulders.

"That date was to be set at your engagement party, which was supposed to be going on tonight." She could hear the stress in her mother's voice. "I won't have you making a mockery of our family, of your father's position. You have one week to get back here, or we'll come down there and drag you home ourselves."

When her phone signaled that her mother had dropped

the call, she sighed and closed her eyes and leaned back against Marcus's shoulder.

"What can I do for you?" he whispered into her hair.

Turning around without a word, she tugged on his hand until he followed her up the stairs. When she reached the landing, she pushed him up against the door and fused her mouth to his.

CHAPTER 15

*M*arcus felt the tension vibrating through her. When her mouth moved over his, he caught up with her. Every bone in his body screamed to be naked with her.

"More…" she demanded as she fumbled behind him trying to get the key in the door, then the door flew open and slammed into the wall.

He spun her around and kicked it shut with his foot. Then she was up against the wall as his hands ran over her.

She tore his shirt from his shoulders, popping out a few buttons along the way. Her mouth was on his skin as his hands fisted in her hair.

"My God," he whispered as her mouth traveled over him. When her hands went to his jeans, he realized he had to take control or he'd lose it too quickly.

Yanking her hands above her head, he held her against the wall and looked down at her. She was so beautiful. He could see anger and hurt in her hazel eyes, but it was the desire he spotted that had him wanting.

He dipped his head and took her mouth again. Her lips told him so much. She was using the want to mask the pain, and he wanted to help her get over the hurt her family had caused.

With her hands still trapped above her, he cupped them in one of his hands so the other could travel down her long body. Her shirt was easy to open. He noticed the tank top underneath. Using his knees, he spread her legs wider and stood between them, rubbing himself against her jeans.

"Is this what you want?" He cupped her and pinched her nipple until it peaked for him. Then he yanked her tank top up and felt her skin against his.

She nodded, and her eyes slid closed as her head fell back against the wall. "Faster," she moaned. "Marcus, I want…" She moaned when he dipped his head and took the erect nipple into his mouth.

Using his teeth, a little, he pleased her until he felt her squirm. Releasing her hands, he yanked her jeans down and turned her so her hands were bracing her up against the wall.

"Yes!" she cried out as his fingers dipped into her heat quickly. She threw her head back as he cupped her and watched her arch her back to give him better access.

She looked too damn good. Her hair was pooled over her shoulders and back as she moaned for him. Her slickness was his undoing. Pulling his pants down, he sheathed himself and then in one quick motion embedded himself into her.

Her cry of joy filled the empty room as he pushed her against the wall with his hips. His fingers reached around and took her erect nipple between his fingers and pinched lightly until he felt her convulse around him.

"More." This time it was him who demanded it.

He could feel her body go lax, so he spun her around and moved forward until she was trapped between him and the wall. Pulling her legs up and around him, he held her against the wall as he continued to pump into her.

He watched her eyes heat all over again. Her legs and arms slowly wrapped around him, holding on as he pumped into her faster. He leaned down and took her mouth and this time when he felt her convulse, he joined her.

The muscles in his arms screamed as he tried to stop them from sliding down the wall. Their breathing was labored and there was a light sheen of sweat running down his back.

"Sorry," he mumbled into her hair.

She laughed. Not just a little chuckle, but a full-blown laugh. As he pulled away from her, he noticed that there were tears in her eyes.

"Oh, God! Did I hurt you?" He rushed closer to her, holding her gently. "I'm sorry," he said again.

She shook her head from side to side. "No." She smiled slightly at him. "It was wonderful. You were wonderful." She ran her finger over his chin. "Really. It's just…" She wiped a tear away from her face. "The call." She closed her eyes. "Everything." She chuckled again as she righted her clothes. "I needed that. I needed you." She looked up at him and he knew exactly what she meant.

"I can't stop needing you." He pulled her close and ran a hand over her hair. "I don't think I want to know what it's like to not need you." He kissed her softly. He desperately wished there was a bed close by, so he could show her exactly how he felt. "Let's go home. I want you again, but this time in a soft bed, so I can make love to you slowly."

"Oh, God!" Her breath hitched, and he watched her eyes heat. "I want you, too."

He took her hand and they walked back to his truck.

"I'm sorry about your folks," he said as he got in and started to pull out of the parking lot.

"It's fine. Really." She kept her eyes glued out the window.

"You can talk to me about it, you know."

She nodded and he waited.

"It's just the same old thing. My whole life it's like I didn't have a voice." She sighed. "I told them I wanted to go to design school, but they sent me to medical school." She closed her eyes and he felt her pain from across the truck. He couldn't imagine what life would have been like if someone had told him he couldn't build or fix things.

"But you went to design school. You're here now." He reached over and took her hand.

"I took some design classes without them knowing. Even put in a few business classes at night." She glanced at him. "I know what's coming and I couldn't ask you to stick around through it."

"I'm not going anywhere." He smiled at her and for the first time since she answered her phone, he saw her smile reach her eyes.

"You say that now but wait until they get here."

He chuckled and squeezed her hand. "I've dealt with worse."

She shook her head and looked out the window again. "Trust me, no you haven't."

❄

Over the next week, she kept busy. She even hired two part-time employees. Marlene was in her early forties and had a very impressive resume. She had two small children and could work during the day. Laura was in her early twenties, had had two previous jobs along the boardwalk, and could work any hours.

The flooring was done in less than two days. Her new shelving and display cases were delivered the following day. Marlene was there during the days to help her organize and tag everything. The woman was quickly becoming invaluable to the business. Not only did she have a wonderful sense of style, but she had a great eye for putting everything where it would look best.

They decided to put all the shoes on the right side and spent half a day hanging the shelving and setting up the display area. It took the other half of the day to tag and display the shoes themselves.

Wendy and Cassey even came down to help her unpack, although Shelly thought that the two had alternative motives when they each bought a bagful of items.

By day four, the place was starting to actually look like a boutique. They had hung the banners and posters from her vendors on the cream-colored walls, which made the place seem warm and inviting.

She had trained the two ladies on the point-of-sale system. Laura was a whiz at it and enjoyed inputting everything.

While Shelly and Marlene set up the items, Laura scanned and entered the items. It was a very efficient system and ended up cutting the setup time in half.

Her evenings were filled with Marcus's family, and the nights with only him. He showed her around, taking her to secluded beaches or dinner at wonderful out-of-the-way restaurants. She loved experiencing new things with him by her side.

They went up to Spring Haven that next weekend and she enjoyed having dinner with his entire family. After eating, they walked out to the lake behind the big house. It was the most romantic spot she'd ever seen. There was a small gazebo built right over the water with large park benches.

"I made this for Julie, so she could enjoy reading on the water," he said, pulling her closer.

"You?" She looked around at the wonderful building. It gave the impression that you were floating over the water. It was so peaceful and romantic that she could imagine spending hours herself enjoying it. There were even soft cushions on the long benches. "You built this?"

He nodded and smiled at her.

"It's wonderful. Your whole family is wonderful." She sighed and tried not to think about the fact that today was the deadline that her mother had set for her to return home.

He cupped her face and must have seen the worry in her eyes. "Don't think about it, about them. Think of only us, here. Now."

Then he bent his head down and took her lips in a kiss that had everything turning foggy.

"I know it may sound crazy." He released a heavy breath, then leaned back and looked at her in the eyes. "But I'm quickly falling in love with you."

She stilled and felt her heart jump in her chest. Shaking

her head from side to side, she closed her eyes. "You… you can't be."

He chuckled and cupped her face again. "It's not the end of the world." He smiled.

She felt tears forming in her eyes. "I… I don't… I can't…"

He stopped her. "You don't have to say or do anything." He kissed her lips, slowly drawing out her anxiety. "Just know that I'm there, and I'm going to enjoy every minute I can with you." He pulled away again and looked at her.

All she could do was nod her head. They walked back to the house and he held her hand. She felt like such a fool. She had strong feelings for him, but love? She'd never experienced that emotion before. With anyone. What did it even feel like to be in love with someone?

She sat in silence as he drove back to his apartment.

"We'll be done with your place in less than a week." He smiled over at her. She had to admit, he was taking her shock at his admission very well. He'd even joked with his brothers and father when they'd said their goodbyes. "I'm sure you'll enjoy having a place all to yourself again. You know, without my brothers always around."

She nodded her head. It would be nice to have her own things around. To have a little privacy again. But she would also miss snuggling up to Marcus every night. Or waking up to him holding her, touching her. She had even enjoyed having his brothers around. She'd always wanted siblings and was beginning to feel like his family was hers. She knew she'd miss it when she moved out.

She closed her eyes on a sigh. "You'll still come around, won't you?" She glanced over at him.

He chuckled. "Just try and keep me away." His eyes sparkled and at that moment, she knew that everything between them was okay.

When they drove up to the apartment, she was shocked to see a large white limo parked out front. Her heart skipped for a second time that night. This time, she doubted it would ever return to a normal beat.

She watched in horror as her mother stepped out of the back, wearing her standard cream dress suit and looking very impatient.

"What do you mean you've cut me off?" Shelly stood in Marcus's living room with her arms crossed over her chest.

Her mother stood in the doorway. She'd briefly glanced around and had yet to acknowledge Marcus even existed, even after Shelly had made the introductions. He had stood with his hand out, ready to shake her mother's hand, but the woman had completely ignored him. Then she'd blurted out that she'd cut Shelly off. He tucked his hands in his pockets and stood back to watch the show. His money was on Shelly winning the argument.

"Well, dear, as you feel that it's important to continue on with this little game of yours, your father and I have decided to cut you off financially."

Shelly laughed. He smiled a little, then started to worry when she continued to laugh even harder. He walked over to her and wrapped an arm around her waist.

"That's rich," she said when her laughter died away. "It's taken you two years and four months to realize that I stopped using a dime of yours and Daddy's money." Shelly crossed her arms over her chest and glared at her mother. "I've been self-sufficient for that long."

He watched her mother's jaw drop a little, but she recovered quickly enough. "Then you'll have no problem if we close your trust fund?"

"By all means, take it all back," she said. He could feel her body vibrating with anger. He dropped his arms and took a step back, not wanting to get singed in the explosion he knew was coming.

"Very well, you leave us no choice. First, you move here against our wishes, then we had to track you down here." Her mother glanced around quickly then down at her perfectly manicured fingernails. "We're officially making the engagement to Tyler Dalton public. Now more than just your friends and family will know about it. Your father will announce it this evening during his speech at the White House."

"Go ahead. I won't honor it." Shelly stood her ground. "I'm not marrying anyone."

Marcus cringed inwardly.

Shelly's mother's face started to turn a shade of pink. "You'll do as you're told. Now…"—she glanced around—"pack whatever bags you have and come home."

"No. I'm not going anywhere."

Her mother stared at her for almost an entire minute, then spun on her heels and left without another word.

He watched Shelly sag a little when the door shut behind her.

Instantly, he was by her side. "Are you okay?" He turned her just as she exploded with tears and threw herself at his chest.

He held her for almost ten minutes before Roman opened the door. He shook his head at his brother and when Roman noticed what was going on, he backed out of the room. His brother actually tiptoed out, shutting the door very quietly behind him. Marcus would have laughed except that Shelly was still crying.

Picking her up, he carried her into his bedroom and toed the door closed behind them. When he laid her on the bed, she didn't even object as he removed her shoes. Then he lay down beside her and held her until he felt her drift off to sleep.

The next morning, he woke when she sat up. She glanced at him and he could see that her eyes were still puffy and red.

"I'm sorry." She looked down at her hands.

He reached over and took her hands and pulled her back down. "Don't. Don't be sorry." He brushed a strand of her hair away from her face. "You have nothing to be sorry for."

"I behaved like a child." She looked over at him and rested her head on his arm.

He chuckled. "The only person who behaved like a child was your mother. When she didn't get what she wanted, she threw a fit."

Shelly chuckled. "My mother has never thrown a fit. She's too well bred for things like that."

"She threw one last night. She wanted you to marry Tyler and when you wouldn't, she took everything she could away from you to get what she wanted." Then he sobered. "Shelly, how are you paying for the store? All the work and products?"

She closed her eyes. "My grandmother left everything

she had to me." Her eyes opened, and he saw pain there. "She left her own daughter nothing."

"That must have pissed off your mother."

Shelly nodded. "That's right about the time she started to push the wedding to Tyler."

He shook his head. "If she can't have it…"

"What?" Shelly frowned.

Marcus laughed. "She's using this marriage to Tyler as her punishment for you. To get even for her mother." Shelly just looked at him. "Don't you see? Since she didn't get her mother's inheritance, she's using a union to Tyler and his family as your punishment."

Shelly shook her head. "My mother may be controlling, but she doesn't care about the money I inherited from my grandmother. Besides, Mom and Dad are so well-off. I mean, what could a measly three hundred thousand more really give them?"

He shook his head. "Just a thought."

She was silent for a while and he could tell she was thinking about it.

"You don't think she'd do anything stupid, do you?" he asked, breaking the silence.

"Like what?"

He shrugged his shoulders. "I dated this girl once…" He watched her eyebrows shoot up, and he couldn't stop from laughing. "Yeah, contrary to what my brothers may have told you, I had other girlfriends before you." He smiled and leaned over to kiss her. "But so far you're the best."

"Continue." She smiled.

"Well, let's just say when I broke it off, my truck suffered some damage."

He saw her eyebrows crease in question.

"She keyed my truck and threw cow manure in the open windows."

Shelly laughed. "What did you do to deserve that? Cheat on her?"

"No!" He leaned back a little. "I don't cheat. If I'm with someone, I'm with that person. If things change…" He shook his head. How had this conversation taken this turn? "Anyway, she was just bitter for a while. In the end, it worked out. She met her husband to be, Jake."

"I don't think my mother would stoop to keying my car, and she would never touch cow manure."

He chuckled. "There are other ways to get back at a person."

He could see Shelly thinking about it. "I don't see how she could do anything. I already have the inspection approved. My business license is hanging up behind the counter." She shook her head. "Everything is ready for me to open next week."

He pulled her close. "Good, then we have nothing to worry about."

Shelly looked at the pile of papers and smiled. This is what she loved about opening her own store. Placing orders. The magazines sat all around her as Marlene looked over her shoulder.

She knew her mother was still in town. The woman hadn't traveled this far to return empty-handed on the first try.

Marcus had probably guessed as much, too. She looked

across the room and saw him hanging the mirrors in the dressing room, a task which should have taken him less than half an hour to complete, but which was going on its third hour.

She liked that without even saying anything, he'd shown her that he would be there for her. She couldn't complain; she liked watching him work.

"What about this one?" Marlene asked, drawing her attention back to the magazine.

"Yes, that's nice," she said absentmindedly.

Marlene chuckled. "You two have it bad."

"Hmm?" She looked over at the woman.

"I remember when my husband and I looked at each other like that." She sighed and rested her chin on her hands.

Shelly looked at Marcus again. He was busy making sure the last mirror was level. His worn jeans hugged him tightly and she remembered exactly what it felt like to get her hands on that tight butt of his. She sighed.

"Love does strange things to us all," Marlene said, causing Shelly to tense slightly. "Now, how about these?" Marlene pointed to the magazine again.

Before she could look down, she saw a movement out of her eye and was completely shocked to see her father walk up to the glass doors and knock on them. Her mother stood by his side.

"Marlene why don't you and Laura take lunch now," she said, not really looking over at the other woman. Her hands shook as she walked across the floor and unlocked the doors, letting her parents in.

"Daddy, I didn't know you were in town." Her voice

sounded a little far away. She cleared her throat to gain a little of her strength back.

"My flight arrived just an hour ago. I came as quickly as I could after your mother told me what was going on." He stepped inside and glanced around the room quickly.

She knew what he was seeing. There were still boxes of product laying around the floor. Half of the hanging products had yet to be steamed or pressed. The shoeboxes were still piled up along the wall instead of being organized in the back area. Basically, the store was a mess, but it was her mess.

Her mother didn't even bother looking around. Instead, her eyes bounced between them, impatiently. She felt like she was eight years old all over again and had just asked if she could stop taking dance classes. This was not going to end well.

Sighing, she motioned for them to move farther into the room. It wouldn't do any good to have potential customers witness what was about to go down.

She walked to the back room, knowing they would follow her. When she stepped inside her office, she turned and was happy to see that Marcus was right behind her.

"Is this where you're staying?" Her father looked around the smaller room with a frown.

"No!" She almost gasped. "My place is upstairs."

"So, you're living upstairs?" Her mother almost sneered.

"Um, no, not yet actually." She bit her bottom lip.

"Shelly, where are you staying?" Her father crossed his arms over his chest, a move he'd used on her countless times.

"Right now I'm staying at Marcus's place." Her chin rose a little in defiance.

Her father sighed. "I suppose I should have expected this." He walked over to the window and shook his head. Then he turned back to her, tilting his head a little. "It's just last-minute jitters."

She gasped. "It's not—"

"Don't speak back to your father." Her mother stepped forward.

Shelly felt deflated and looked down at her hands. It was an old emotion, feeling small around them.

"I've explained to the Daltons. They've agreed to postpone the wedding until you're up to it." Shelly bit back a remark. "Now, are you ready to leave?"

She didn't know exactly what she was saying in the next few moments, only that her entire body vibrated with every word. Her voice rose, and she dug her fingernails into her palms so much that the pain shook her out of the trance.

"Easy," Marcus said in her ear. "Take a breath."

She closed her eyes and did as he said. She felt his hand in hers and focused on how good it felt. "I won't be going anywhere." She looked directly at her father. "I plan on staying in Surf Breeze forever."

The room was silent, and she realized both of her parents were staring at her like they'd never seen her before.

"Clearly you're having some sort of breakdown," her father said, walking towards her slowly with his hands up.

"Be careful, Gerald," her mother said. Shelly almost laughed. What? Did the woman think she would bite?

"I'm perfectly fine. For once in *my* life, I'm doing what *I* want. I want to be in Surf Breeze. I want to live with Marcus." She turned to him and gave him a smile, which he quickly returned. "I love it here." She turned back to her parents.

Her father stopped and looked at her. "What are we going to tell the Daltons?"

Shelly shrugged her shoulders. "You don't have to say anything to them. I broke it off with Tyler almost two months ago. He's a big boy; he can break the news to his own parents."

Her father looked like he was thinking about the situation. He sighed. "Well, looks like I need to have a little talk with Tyler." He turned to her mother. "Come on Cherease, we have a call to make."

It shocked her to see her mother smile and follow her father through the front doors.

"Did they just give up?" Marcus asked from beside her.

She sighed. "God! I hope so." She closed her eyes on all the pain. "They didn't even comment on my store."

He pulled her close and brushed his hands through her hair. She loved it when he did that, when he touched her softly, making her feel cherished.

"From where I'm standing, they don't deserve you." He rested his forehead against hers as the tears started to fall down her cheeks.

He pulled her closer as she let the hurt and pain show. "Why can't they just accept me for who I am? It's like they don't even see me. All they see is a pawn to be moved around and sacrificed."

He shook his head and held her close. "Trust me,

sometimes it's better to wash your hands completely of people who don't believe in you."

She pulled back and looked at him. "Like you did with your parents? Your real ones, I mean."

He nodded slowly. "You can't even imagine what life was like for me. Not that you don't have it bad." He closed his eyes and sighed. "Sorry."

She shook her head. "No, I understand. I'd love to hear about it. Go on."

He looked around. "How about we go sit in a dark booth at Cassey's and have a beer. I could use a beer to get through this story."

She nodded. She could use a beer too, maybe even two.

"I'll leave a note for Marlene and Laura telling them to take the rest of the day off."

He smiled. "Now you're talking."

"I was five years old, almost six when my mom's new boyfriend first started abusing me." He looked at her across the table and felt his stomach roll. He'd never talked about it, not to anyone before, not even his father or brothers. No one knew the silent pain he'd gone through. But something in him wanted—no, needed —to tell Shelly. Especially after today. She had to know what she was committing herself to.

"I'm sorry." She frowned and took another sip of her beer. "It must have been horrible."

He nodded. "Not the kind of abuse you're thinking." He waited and watched acknowledgment cross her eyes. Her hand quickly reached across the table and took his.

"Oh my God!" It came out as a whisper.

"Eight months. Most of my very first memories are of what he did to me on an almost nightly basis." He watched tears come to Shelly's eyes again and blocked out the memories that threatened to drown him. "At first I was too young to really understand. I listened to his bull about it being a game and a secret." He closed his eyes, then opened them again and took a large drink of his beer so he would have the guts to finish the story.

"How'd you get away?" Her hand felt cold and smooth in his. When he looked down at their joined fingers, he was amazed at the difference between them. Her pale skin was perfect, and his darker hands showed signs of hard work. Suddenly, he didn't feel good enough for her. He wanted to pull his hand away and shove it in his pockets, but she held it firm.

"I didn't get away as much as was abandoned." He heard her gasp. "One night my mother was watching the news. There was a report of a woman who had stabbed a man that had broken into her house to rape her. After Mom left to go to work, I took the biggest knife we had in the apartment and hid it under my pillow." His eyes were focused on her hands as he talked. He couldn't bear to see the pain and sympathy in her eyes. "The first time he woke me that night, I was too afraid." He shook his head. "I'd been asleep and had forgotten about the knife. But sometimes he would come back a second time, and this time I was waiting for him. I stabbed him six times." He looked up at her when she gasped again. "I didn't kill him. Actually, I didn't do much damage. It took my mother less than five minutes to fix him up. He was more pissed than anything. I remember sitting in the corner holding the bloody knife, thinking I should have tried harder." He looked back down at their hands. She'd tightened her grip on him and he was thankful. It was almost like an anchor, holding him to the present. "When I told my mother why I'd stabbed Mike, she slapped me and called me a liar. The next week, she drove me to the boys' home and signed the paperwork, dissolving her rights to me." He blinked and was shocked to see a tear fall onto his hand. He looked up and realized it was his. Shaking his head, he smiled a little. "It was the second-best thing that has happened to me." He looked at her face and felt all of the bad memories fade away.

"Marcus…" She shook her head and closed her eyes. "I had no idea…" She looked at him and he could see the pain in her eyes. "My parents look like saints now." She chuckled nervously.

"Don't," he said in a low voice. When she looked up at him with questions in her eyes, he continued. "Don't pity me. Like I said, it was the best thing that could have happened to me, getting away from that evil. You did the same thing by coming here." He reached over and took her other hand. "You took your own life in your hands and decided to start over." He smiled. "If I was half as strong as—"

Her chuckle interrupted him. "Half as strong… You were stronger at six than I am at twenty-four." She shook her head. "I can only hope to be as strong as you one day."

He smiled. "You were today." She looked up at him and smiled back. "Freaking Xena the warrior, facing off with her mortal enemies."

"Who?" She blinked up at him and he laughed.

"Okay, I see a whole weekend and a stack of DVDs in our future." He laughed some more when she just smiled at him. "You are every inch a warrior princess, and I was so proud of you today."

Her smile brightened and then quickly changed as she looked down at their hands. "I just hope it did the trick."

"If not, I'm sure you can stand up against anything."

"With you by my side, I feel like I can." She got up and crossed over to sit next to him. When she reached up and placed a soft kiss on his lips, he realized he'd been denying the depth of his feelings for her.

Looking into her eyes, he felt something loosen in his chest. "I love you." It came out as a whisper and he felt her tense in his arms. "No, don't tense." He used the back of his fingers and brushed them up against her soft cheek. "Listen to me. Look at me. I run a construction business in a small beach community. I'm no high-powered businessman with fancy cars, fancy houses. I've got a pretty screwed-up past, but a wonderful family that I wouldn't trade for the world, and I love you. Completely. Wholly. Painfully. I'm not asking you to—"

"I love you too," she interrupted. When his eyes moved to hers, he saw that she was telling the truth. "I can't believe it happened so quickly, but there it is. I've been denying it for days." She sighed and shook her head. "Weeks actually."

He chuckled. "Me too." He rubbed a finger over her wet cheek.

"I've never felt this way about anyone before." She sighed.

"So, you've said." He pulled her closer and enjoyed the way she fit against him. "What do you say to eating some food and then clocking off early? I'd like to drive by the place on Sugar Sand Lane and take another look at it with you. I've got the code, so we can take our time looking."

She pulled away and smiled up at him. "I'd love to."

"Good, because I hope you know, I plan on making it

our place. If you'll move in with me once it's finished, that is."

She smiled. "I'd love to."

When they drove up the driveway, he couldn't stop himself from smiling. His mind was whirling with ideas and plans for the place.

"Tell me what you're envisioning," Shelly said beside him.

He glanced over at her and nodded, then proceeded to tell her all his ideas. As they walked through the place, he told her his plans. He even sketched out the kitchen for her as they stood at the island.

When they stepped out onto the back deck, he wrapped his arms around her and pulled her closer. There was a light breeze coming off the water and she shivered in his arms.

"We should have grabbed your coat." He kissed the top of her head.

"I'm okay as long as you have your arms around me." She rested her head back against his chest and he could imagine them standing here like this for the rest of their lives.

The next day Marlene, Laura, and Shelly had to play catch up. Marcus had been called off early to another job. But he hadn't left her until she'd promised to call him if her parents showed up.

She doubted they would, but she knew the fight wasn't over. She'd logged into her bank and changed her security information, removing them as her emergency contact.

She'd noticed that her trust fund was blocked to her, but she didn't care. As long as they couldn't touch her inheritance from Nanna, she was fine. She had plans to call the bank later today to make sure that they couldn't.

It took the three of them all morning to finish setting up the store. By the time lunch rolled around, the place was looking great. There were still a few items that had to be tagged, but for the most part, they were ready to open the doors.

The man had come and installed her credit card line and machine earlier that day, and she was very eager to try it out on the first sale.

Marlene and Laura left to grab some lunch, so she stood in the store and soaked up everything. Her eyes scanned every detail, from the color of the walls to the warm rich feeling of the floors, the bright-colored clothes that hung on the racks and the shoes that shined on the wall. She would have loved to shop at a place like this.

Sighing, she turned and almost bumped solidly into someone.

"Oh!" She gasped when she saw Tyler frowning down at her. His hands were on her shoulders, keeping her from falling over. "Tyler?" She frowned and wished more than anything that she'd anticipated her parents making this move. "What are you doing here?"

He dropped his hands and she watched his left eyebrow rise in question. "I came because your parents asked me to." Even though his voice was calm, she knew it could rise higher with anger.

"They shouldn't have called you." She crossed her arms over her chest. She desperately wished to take a step back, but she wasn't going to give him that satisfaction. "I meant it when I ended it between us."

He nodded slightly. "Well, I understand, but our parents have a different agenda for us. It looks like we'll be going through with the wedding after all."

She sighed. "I'm not marrying you. You know that." She flinched a little when his hands went back to her shoulders and tightened on her arms.

One of the reasons she'd broken off the relationship was his recent behavior. She didn't like to be dominated. He had started to act differently, demanding to know where she was, what she was doing at all times. He'd never hit her, but he had yelled and cussed and said some hurtful things to her.

"Listen, I dislike the plan as much as you do, but I'm not going to jeopardize my inheritance or yours." He turned and started walking towards the door. "So, we'll just go tell them the wedding is back on."

At this point, he was almost dragging her out of the front doors. She was so shocked at his behavior; she didn't think to pull away.

But when the cool air hit her face outside, she woke up. Tugging her arms free, she took a few steps away from him.

"I'm not marrying you. I don't care about my inheritance or yours." She watched his face turn a dark shade of red.

"Shelly, this is neither the time nor the place to have this discussion. Besides, it's too late. You've already agreed to the wedding and if you don't go through with it, my parents are prepared to sue yours for breach of contract."

"Breach of contract?" she squealed. "What are you

talking about? I didn't sign any contract. Nor would my parents."

"Verbal contract." Tyler smiled.

Shelly laughed. "Oh, that's rich." She crossed her arms over her chest. "Is that why your parents are pressuring mine? What do they hope to gain from our marriage?"

He stood there looking at her like she'd grown an extra head.

"What was the plan?" She waited, thinking. "Go ahead, try and sue. It won't stand up in court. Actually, I'm pretty sure you'll get laughed at by every lawyer." Tyler chuckled and raised that damn eyebrow of his again.

Then she gasped inwardly when she remembered what Tyler's father did for a living. She doubted even a high-powered lawyer like him would win a case like that. She continued to stand her ground.

"You can make it easier on your family by just going along." He reached out and took her arm in a vice grip again. "Imagine the rumors and scandals we can have floating around about you and your family. Your father will be ruined."

"Get your hands off my daughter." She heard anger in her father's voice that she'd never heard before. She turned and watched her parents step closer. She hadn't realized they'd been standing a few feet away. When she blinked, she noticed Marcus and Roman standing behind them a little way. Marcus looked like he was about to tear Tyler in half, but Roman was holding his arms pretty tightly.

"Dad?" Her father marched over to where she stood, standing between her and Tyler.

"If you ever get near my family again, I'll hire a better lawyer than your father and sue your entire family right out of Washington. Have I made myself clear?" He waited until Tyler backed down and nodded. "Now, I don't care what you tell your family about what happened here, but I will be making an official announcement later tonight about the engagement being off. If I were you, I'd hop on the earliest flight out."

Shelly watched as Tyler rushed down the boardwalk towards the parking lot. Then she turned and was immediately engulfed in Marcus's arms.

"Are you okay?" When she just nodded, he pushed back and gently moved her sleeves up her arms. When she looked, she noticed red rings around both of them where Tyler's hands had grabbed her. "I'll kill him…" Marcus moved to follow the man to the parking garage.

"Don't, son." Her father shocked her by putting a hand on his shoulder. "I've kicked him where it counts." He shook his head and frowned down at the marks on her arms. "Unless Shelly wants to file charges?"

Shelly shook her head. She just wanted it all to be over with.

"Let's get you inside," Roman said, taking her arm gently. "You must be freezing out here without a coat."

She hadn't even realized that she was shivering. Nodding her head, she allowed Marcus and Roman to lead her inside while her parents followed them.

"Do you want some water?" Roman asked.

She shook her head no and rubbed her hands together. Marcus walked over and yanked one of the new sweaters off a hanger and set it gently over her shoulders. "Put your arms through this to warm up."

"Marcus, this is a…" She started to object to using a sweater that was for sale in her own store.

"Shush." He frowned. "Just put it on."

She put her arms through the warm material and sighed. It was soft, and she had to admit, she'd been eyeing the sweater for herself ever since it had arrived.

"Shelly?" She turned towards her mother, who had tears silently streaming down her face. "I…" She shook her head and closed her eyes. "I thought it was for the best. I didn't realize…"

Shelly's father moved closer to her mother and wrapped his wife in his arms. It was the first time Shelly had seen him do that in over ten years.

"Shhh, Cherease, we were all fooled by them."

"They made it sound like she was having a nervous breakdown." Her mother hiccupped and rested her head against her husband's shoulder as she closed her eyes. Just the sight of her parents like that brought back so many memories of the good times they used to have. Her heart ached for them again.

"Who?" Shelly frowned.

Her father looked over at her. "Shortly after you left, we received a call from the Daltons. They spun a story about how you'd sold everything, that you'd given someone all your money, and you were living in a dump. Tyler mentioned something about your mental health. We just assumed…" He broke off with a frown.

"Just what do you think I'm doing down here? Living like a bum?"

"Well, you are living in a small apartment with two strange men," her mother added, looking down her nose at her.

Shelly started to laugh. "Look around," she finally said when she got her voice back. "What do you see?"

Her father glanced around. "A store. We assumed you worked here." He shook his head. "All those years at college, wasted."

Marcus laughed then. "Sorry." He cleared his throat.

Shelly nodded and smiled at him. "First off, the men I live with are no more strangers to me than you two are. They're family." She smiled over at them both and was rewarded with twin nods. "I'm just living with them until my apartment is finished, then I plan on asking Marcus to move in with me until we can close on his house and have the renovations done. Then I plan on living with him in a beautiful house on the beach." She watched her mother's eyebrows rise but didn't stop to let them ask any questions. "Second, I do work here." She crossed her arms over her chest and smiled. "But I also own it. Shelly's Boutique is going to be the best store along the boardwalk, and I open my doors in less than a week." She watched with pleasure as both of her parents took another look around.

"This?" her mother said. "This is yours?" They were looking at everything as if for the first time, taking in how wonderful it all looked. She smiled. It did look wonderful.

Shelly nodded. "Didn't you see the sign above the door?"

They both shook their heads no. "We were too busy trying to figure out how to drag you home, so we could hire a very good psychologist."

Marcus laughed again. "Sorry, again." He cleared his throat once more.

"Mom, Dad." Shelly took a deep breath. "Let's start over. Shall we?" They both nodded. "Good. I'd like to introduce you to Marcus and Roman Grayton. They own a very successful construction business as well as a halfway house where orphaned or unwanted children can live until they can be adopted." She walked over and put her arms around Marcus's waist as he wrapped his around her shoulders. "Marcus is my boyfriend. We're in love and are going to move in with each other."

Marcus held out his hand and shook her father's hand, then her mother's.

"It's a pleasure to meet you," her father said, and she realized with glee that he actually meant it.

CHAPTER 18

"I'm so nervous," Shelly said, trying to stop her hands from shaking.

"Don't be, it'll be perfect. Just wait and see." Marlene smiled.

"Shall I?" Laura asked, nodding towards the front doors.

"No, I'll do it." Shelly took up the keys and walked towards the glass doors. She could see the small crowd that had gathered out front. It took her two tries to finally slide the key into the lock and flip it. Then she took a deep breath, turned on the open sign, and stood back as people rushed in.

She smiled when she saw her mother walk in with Cassey and Wendy. Her parents had decided to stay until after opening day to support her. They had booked a suite at Luke's resort and had even planned to come back during the official season, so they could enjoy an actual vacation.

"I can't believe how beautiful this place is," Cassey

said as she hugged her. "Your mother is being a gem," she whispered in her ear.

Shelly had warned Cassey about her mother and had asked her to keep her posted. But so far, her parents were being extra nice, especially to one another. She could only hope that the whole ordeal had brought them closer together.

She had spent hours talking with them, getting everything off her chest about how they'd alienated her over the last years. How had the strain in their relationship bled over to her? They had sat silently at first, listening to her. Then they had broken down and started to open up about the troubles they were having. In the end, she felt closer to them. But it wouldn't completely clear the slate until they proved to her that she was important to them again.

The next hours were busy. She and Marlene and Laura rushed around and helped customers. There was a slight lull around lunch, but it quickly picked up again and stayed busy until closing time. When Shelly walked back to the doors and locked them, she rested her forehead on the glass and smiled.

"Well," Laura said from behind her, "I'd say that was a successful first day." She laughed.

Shelly turned around and looked at the store. It was a good thing she had more boxes in the back to be opened. She could see a lot of empty places that would need to be filled by tomorrow.

"I told you it would be great." Marlene smiled.

Just then there was a knock on the door. When she turned around, she could only see a very large bundle of white roses.

Unlocking the door with a smile, she took them from

Marcus and buried her face in them, drinking in their scent.

"They're beautiful." She smiled at him.

"Not as beautiful as you." He moved the flowers to the side and wrapped his arms around her and kissed her. "How'd it go today?"

"Perfect." She couldn't stop smiling. "How did it go with you?"

He smiled and held up a set of keys and shook them. "I'm a homeowner."

She squealed and hugged him again. "Congratulations."

He chuckled. "How long will it take you to close up?"

She glanced back and calculated. "An hour."

He nodded. "What do you say to dinner at..." He nodded towards the bar and grill.

"I'd love it. I'm starved."

"Good, I'll meet you down there." He leaned down and kissed her again.

"Okay, see you then."

She walked into the back room and placed the roses in a vase with water and set them on her desk. They really were beautiful.

It took her less than an hour to close out and prepare her deposits. She was shocked at the amount they'd taken in that day. She knew that opening week was bound to be more successful than normal days, but still, if she made half of what they had today, she was going to be happy.

When she walked into the bar and grill, she was a little shocked to see the entire back dance area blocked off. Three large tables were moved together and everyone she knew and cared about was there. Marcus's father and his sister Julie sat next to her own parents.

Marcus rushed over to her as everyone cheered and greeted her.

"A toast." Cassey stood up and held up a wine glass filled with her standard drink, a Coke. "To the first of many successful days at Shelly's Boutique." She was handed a glass and drank as everyone cheered.

Her heart was so full, she felt like it was about to burst.

Dinner was loud and filled with good food and wonderful people. She wouldn't have changed a thing. Shortly after she'd finished eating, Marcus leaned close to her.

"I do have one more surprise for you," he whispered. "What do you say to getting out of here?"

She nodded and felt heat rush through her. Would the man always make her knees go weak with just the richness of his voice?

She held his hand as he walked her to the parking lot and helped her into his truck.

"I hope you don't mind leaving your party early?" He frowned a little.

She shook her head no. "It's been a busy day. I'm happy to have the quiet." She rested her head back against the headrest as he drove.

She hadn't realized she'd closed her eyes until he stopped the truck. Her eyes flew open and she noticed that they were parked outside of his new house.

"I know it's not much to look at now." He turned to her. "But it will be soon."

She nodded, looking at the place. "It's wonderful and it's all yours."

He chuckled. "Yeah." He turned and looked at the house with her. "I promise; this will be good." He smiled as he walked around and opened her door for her.

She nodded and followed him up the stairs. When he opened the door, he stood back and let her enter first.

She'd forgotten how great the place was. She walked into the large foyer and looked through the large windows in the great room that overlooked the beach.

The sun was just setting, filling the sky with pastel colors and lighting up the entire room.

She looked down and saw a massive blanket and unlit candles on the floor. There was a bowl of strawberries and a bottle of champagne that was being chilled.

"Oh, it's perfect." She smiled over at him as he shut the door behind them.

"I hope you don't mind, but I wanted to see if you'd be up to staying here tonight. I brought your air mattress and your overnight bag."

She walked over to him and wrapped her arms around his shoulders. "It's perfect."

He pulled back and then took her hand as he walked over to the blanket. He helped her sit down and then opened the champagne. She held her glass up and he filled it and then his own.

She loved the sound of it fizzing and waited until he sat next to her before holding her glass up. "To new beginnings."

He nodded and smiled, then drank a little.

"Here, have some of this." He handed her the bowl of strawberries. When she took one, he held up the bowl of cream for her to dip it in.

"Mmmm." She closed her eyes and enjoyed the taste. "Perfect."

When she opened her eyes, she saw him watching her lips and her insides tightened.

"Marcus?" She set her glass down, then took his and set it next to her own. "I want you," she whispered as she knelt in front of him.

He nodded slowly. "I…" He shook his head. Then blinked. "You make me forget everything," he said, pulling back a little.

She smiled. "That's a good thing."

"Normally." He nodded and smiled. Then he cleared his throat and held up the bowl of strawberries again. "Here, one more."

She shook her head. "It's you I want."

He frowned a little. "Just one more?"

Something in his eyes made her nod and reach for another berry.

Marcus held his breath as her hand brushed up against the cold metal. He'd been so sure that she'd see it right away, but she was too busy looking at him.

Maybe he wasn't doing this right? He sighed when she took another juicy berry to her lips. Damn!

He couldn't keep from watching her lips as she took the pink berry between them and nibbled on it. He felt his groin grow hard and he almost forgot his carefully laid out plan.

Reaching into the bowl himself, he pulled out his mother's ring and held it up.

"Shelly Harrison, I can't seem to do anything right without you." He shook his head. That isn't what he'd wanted to say. "Shelly," he tried again, "I love you. I don't want to live another day without the joy of falling asleep and waking up with you in my arms. Say you'll not only move in here with me but that you'll marry me."

She looked down at the ring and frowned a little. "I…" She shook her head and rested back on her feet. "I… I don't know what to say."

He smiled. "I'd love to hear a 'yes' right about now."

He watched the corners of her mouth turn up a little. Her eyes were glued to the ring he held in front of her. Taking her hand, he waited, holding the ring, ready to slide it into place.

"Marcus?" she said as her eyes went to his, and for a moment, his heart dropped. "I know this is sudden. I mean, it's all happened so fast." She shook her head and for a moment, he thought she was going to turn him down. Then she launched herself at him and was kissing him and he knew he had his answer.

He pulled back a little and slid the ring on her finger. Her eyes didn't leave his. He pulled her close and kissed her until he felt himself falling back as she straddled him.

Her hands pulled on his clothes as he tugged on hers. When they were finally gloriously naked, he flipped them, so he could look down at her sprawled underneath him. Her hair fanned out on the blanket as he smiled down at her.

"I'm glad you changed your mind." He trailed a finger down her neck slowly.

"Hmmm?" She closed her eyes and he felt her move under him.

"About not marrying anyone ever." His finger circled her skin as it puckered for him.

"I never meant you." Her eyes opened. "You're the only man I could ever imagine myself marrying." Her hands came up and pulled on him until their lips touched gently. "The only man I'd ever want to marry."

He couldn't stop the smile. "You're the only woman I could see being with. The only one I've ever opened myself completely to."

"I love you."

"I love you, too," he said and placed a soft kiss on her lips and then took it deeper until they were both breathless.

"You're killing me," she moaned as he felt her hips jerk next to him. She wrapped her legs around his hips and tugged on him until he moved closer.

When he slid into her, it was like coming home. She fit him like she was the missing piece he'd been searching for his entire life. Her body was soft and welcoming, and he knew he'd never get used to knowing that she'd chosen him.

He made love to her slowly as the moon rose over the Gulf. They fell asleep in their new house tangled together, knowing that they'd found each other.

EPILOGUE

Shelly felt the evening breeze from where she sat. Even though the day had been a scorcher, the breeze off the water cooled the crowd as the sun sunk slowly over the water.

When the music started, she turned and watched the bride walk across the soft sand. Cassey's long hair was loose around her face in tight little ringlets. Her white dress flowed around her in soft waves, hugging all the right places.

She'd met Luke's father and mother and had enjoyed meeting the other guests that sat around her. When the crowd stood, Shelly's eyes went to Marcus's and she couldn't stop smiling at him as he stared at his sister walking down the aisle.

He looked so very handsome in his cream-colored suit standing next to his other brothers.

It had been almost four months since she'd opened Shelly's. When she'd moved to her dream beach, she'd never imagined that she'd find herself being taken in by a dream family.

She sat back down and watched Cassey and Luke proclaim their love for one another and her eyes misted. Her eyes and her mind kept wandering to the man she loved and planned on marrying within the next year.

There was still so much to do before her own date. Her parents had talked them into hosting two weddings, one in DC with all the "right" people and another one here, on their very own beach.

They had both agreed to wait until the house was finished.

Her boutique was a huge success. When the official season had started, she'd quickly realized that two part-time employees wouldn't work, so she had hired Marlene as a full-time manager and had hired two more part-time employees.

When the bride and groom walked back down the sandy aisle together, all smiles, she cheered with the rest of the guests.

The reception was held at the bar and grill. She enjoyed dancing with Marcus on the dance floor and had even danced with the groom and Marcus's brothers.

She'd never witnessed anything so exciting as his family coming together to celebrate. She doubted the reception her mother was planning for them would be anything like what she'd experienced that evening. She was planning on having her party, here, just like this one, with loud people laughing and joking and having a great time.

As Marcus claimed her for another dance, she pulled

close to him and enjoyed his kisses as he spun her on the dance floor to the slow music. As she enjoyed the feeling of him twirling her around and making her heart race, she knew without a doubt that it was exactly where she wanted to be for the rest of her life.

PROLOGUE

Hot wind whirled around Lauren's skirt, causing it to fly up. She laughed as she twirled around. Stopping for a second to catch her breath, she looked over at her sisters, Alex and Haley. Alex's bright blonde head was pointed downward as she sat in the dirt, happily making a mud pile. Haley's dark curly hair lay in the grass as she watched the clouds rush by.

Lauren looked up at the sky and noticed that the clouds were going by very fast. Frowning a little, she decided that dancing some more while keeping her eyes glued to the sky might be fun. She twirled while watching everything rush by her, almost causing her to tumble over and fall.

Dancing in the fields was one of her greatest joys. Even though she had to babysit her younger sisters today, she didn't mind. For the most part, her sisters could entertain themselves. Lauren still had to carry Haley sometimes when her short legs got tired. She supposed that being four was tiring, though she couldn't remember ever being four. She thought she must have slept through her life until she turned five when her first memories happened. Haley was always asleep, or lying down, like now. But Lauren was eight and she had enough energy to shake the roof off the barn, or so her Daddy always said.

The breeze moved the tall grass around them, making the field look as if it were dancing with her. She stopped to bow to her make-believe dance partner, a move she'd seen late one night when she had sneaked to the edge of the stairs. Her parents had been watching an old black-and-white movie and she could make out the screen if she tilted her head just right. The woman in the long white dress had bowed slowly while smiling at a tall gentleman in a black suit and tie. They'd looked so wonderful. From that moment on, Lauren had wanted to dance. Every chance she had, she'd moved around like she'd watched the couple do, wishing her dress was longer so it would flow like the ladies had.

Taking a break, she looked off towards the house. The large three-story stone place sat like a beacon in the yellow fields. Its bright white pillars gleamed in the sunlight, at least when the clouds weren't shadowing the land. It was the only place she'd ever known as home. Her dad's dad had built the place a long, long time ago. Probably a zillion years ago. The outside looked new, and her dad did everything he could to keep the inside looking new, too. But Lauren knew some of the floorboards creaked when you walked on them. And the water only stayed hot long enough for her and her sisters to share a bath at night. But worst of all, she had blue carpet in her bedroom. Lauren hated blue. She'd begged her dad for new carpet, yellow preferably. Her dad told her it was blue because it used to be his room, and that it would have to stay blue until they could afford new carpet. Her room was perfect, except for the blue carpet. It was like a big wart on her room. Not that she'd ever gotten warts. Jenny Steven's had a wart once on her finger and she had to wear a My Little Pony Band-Aid over it. But during recess, Jenny had pulled the Band-Aid off and shown Lauren her wart. It was gross, all wet and puffy. So, Lauren thought of her blue carpet as a wart on the face of her bedroom.

Looking at the house, she knew her mama was back in the kitchen making a feast for the church potluck tomorrow. Everyone was going to be there, even Dale Bennett. She didn't like Dale; he always pulled her hair and pushed her into the dirt, even when she was wearing her new church dress.

She knew that her mama was the best cook in the county. Or so her daddy always said.

Hearing a loud noise, she looked off towards the dark clouds that were forming over the hills. Her daddy was somewhere up in the hills, gathering the cows. She didn't know why they had to move the cows around all the time. It was still a mystery to her why they couldn't just stay here in the fields. There was plenty of tall grass to eat right here, close to the house. Another loud sound came from the hills. At first, Lauren thought it was a gunshot. She'd heard a lot of those growing up on the huge ranch, but then she turned her head a little and heard her mother screaming for them.

"Girls! Run, come quick!" Her mother stood in the front door, her apron flowing in the wind as her hands motioned for them to come to her.

"Come on. Mama wants us to run," Lauren told her sisters.

Alex stood and dusted off her hands and started skipping towards the house. Haley, on the other hand, didn't move.

"Come on, Haley, Mama wants us to run home." Another loud noise came from behind her and when she looked, the sky had turned black. Fear shot through her like a bolt of lightning. Without saying a word, Lauren grabbed up her baby sister and started running. Since her legs were longer than Alexis', she made it to her skipping sister and screamed for her to run faster. Halfway to the house, Lauren had to set Haley down. Her little sister had gained a few pounds and was too heavy for her to carry the entire way. Their mother wasn't in the doorway when they got there; instead, she was standing in the hallway.

"Quick, we have to get to the shelter." Her mother picked up Haley and started running towards the back door.

"Mama, Bear!" Haley screamed. "I want Bear!"

Their old deaf dog was lying by the fireplace, where he always stayed, taking a nap.

"Fine." Their mother set Haley down next to her and looked Lauren in the eyes. At this time, Lauren could hear the wind rushing through the house. The sound was so loud that Haley covered her ears and started to cry. "Lauren, I want you to make sure you get your sisters into the shelter like I taught you. Can you do that?"

Lauren remembered the drills Mama and Papa had put her through. Nodding her head, she grabbed her sisters' hands. "Yes, Mama."

"Good. Now run," her mother yelled over the noise, then she took off down the hallway to grab the dog as Lauren turned and started running, dragging her sisters behind her. When they got to the kitchen, Alex stopped. She pulled her hand out of Lauren's and started grabbing cookies that their mother had been baking.

"No, Alex, we have to go now." Lauren dropped Haley's hand and grabbed Alex by the shoulders, causing her to drop all the cookies.

"No, I'm gonna tell Mama." Alex started crying. Here in the back of the house, the noise was even louder. She could see grass and leaves fly by the windows when she looked out.

"We have to get to the shelter, or Mama is going tell Daddy." That stopped her sister from picking up the dropped cookies. Lauren grabbed her hand and turned back to get Haley, but Haley was gone. Just then their mother came into the kitchen carrying the old dog.

"Where's Haley?" she screamed, as she held the old dog in her arms.

"I don't know. She was just here. Then Alex—"

"Here, we don't have time for stories now. Take Bear and Alex and get to the shelter. Run girls, run!" Her mother pushed Bear into her arms. The dog looked small in her mother's arms, but in hers, he was heavy. She had to shift his fat body to make sure she didn't drop him. Alex ran to the back door and opened it. Hearing her mother's urgent tone, she must have understood that something bad was happening.

The girls rushed across the backyard through the high wind and the heavy rain that was falling. When they reached the storm shelter, Lauren had to set Bear down to open the big door. Alex grabbed Bear's collar, making sure he didn't run away as Lauren pushed the door open. Then Alex pulled Bear down the stairs as Lauren looked back towards the house. She could see a light go on in her sister's bedroom, then her mother's shadow crossed the window. Her mother bent down, and when she stood back up, Lauren could see that Haley was in her arms. She felt relieved until she looked up.

"Run, Mama!" Lauren screamed. The dark clouds circled above the house, and Lauren's little body froze to the spot outside the shelter. It seemed like hours later when her mother finally appeared at the back door holding Haley. Her sister's head was buried in her mother's apron.

"Get inside!" her mother screamed halfway across the backyard.

Lauren's feet became unglued and she rushed to the bottom of the stairs. Turning, she waited for her mother to reach the shelter door. She watched as her mother's dress flew sideways in the high winds. Haley was holding onto her apron tightly.

Then everything slowed down in Lauren's mind. Her mother, a few steps from the doorway, looked up quickly, then turned her head and looked right at her. Lifting Haley high, she threw her into the open doorway. Haley fell down the stairs, and her little body hit Lauren's with enough force that it knocked them down. Haley's body shook as she cried, still clutching a piece of their mother's apron, which had been ripped from her shoulders. Lauren quickly got up and stood on the floor of the shelter, looking up into the doorway. She watched in terror as the ferocious winds ripped her mother from the doorway and swept her into the darkness.

LOVING LAUREN

CHAPTER 1

Ten years later…

Lauren looked down at the grave as a tear slipped down her nose. It was a week before her nineteenth birthday, and she watched as her father's closest friends lowered his casket into the ground. She heard her sisters crying beside her and blindly reached over and took both of their hands. It had been two days since she'd found her father lying on his bedroom floor. She'd done everything she'd known to try and save him, but she'd been too late. She'd do anything to go back and somehow get to the house earlier that sunny day.

Closing her eyes, she could remember her father's face, his kindness, the way he moved and smelled, and the way he talked. Everything about the man had told his daughter's that he loved them, that he'd do anything for them. They'd lost their mother ten years ago; their father had picked up the pieces and raised three girls on his own. They had all missed their mother, but thanks to their father, they had grown up knowing that they were loved. They had never gone to bed hungry, dirty, or without a bedtime story.

If the food had been a little burnt or a little odd tasting, the girls never complained. Even when Alex's costume for the school play had turned out looking more like a green leaf than a tree, she hadn't complained. When Lauren had finally hit the age to legally drive, she'd taken it upon herself to drive her sisters to and from school and any other after school functions they'd been involved in, even if it meant forgoing her own social life.

The guilt had always played in the back of her mind. *If I had just watched Haley better. If I had just kept holding her hand, Mama would be here today.*

The school had offered the girls counseling, but Lauren had just sat through it and had told the older woman who had been assigned to counsel her what she'd wanted to hear. Not once did she hint that it was her fault that their mother was gone. Not once did she confide in anyone that she was to blame.

When her father was in the ground, she closed her eyes and lifted her face to the sky. The spring Texas air felt wonderful. She knew that in a little over a month, the breeze would be hot enough to steam the tears that were falling down her face. The cool wind would stop and be replaced by stillness and heat. But for now, she enjoyed the smell of the grass growing, the flowers blooming, and the sight of the cherry trees that were planted around the small cemetery. Her father had always loved the spring. He'd been looking forward to helping her plant a new flower garden near the back of the house.

Now, who was she going to plant flowers with? She opened her eyes and looked at Alexis. Her blonde hair was tied up in a simple bun at the base of her neck. Her black skirt and gray shirt were in complete contrast to her sister's normal attire. Even though Alex had just turned sixteen, her wild side had been on the loose for the last two years. So much so that it had started eating up a lot of Lauren's and their father's time.

"Your sister is going to be the death of me. Mark my words, Lauren. Someday you're going to walk in and she'll be standing over my cold body, complaining about the fact that she can't have a pair of hundred-dollar jeans."

In fact, Alex hadn't been home that day. She'd stayed the night at a friend's house that entire weekend.

Lauren looked over at Haley. She was too young to remember their mother. And even though they'd never talked about it, she knew her sister was a little jealous of the fact that Lauren and Alex could both remembered her.

As the minister, a longtime family friend was saying his closing, Lauren looked down at her father's final resting place. What was she going to do now? How were they going to live without him?

Her shoulders sank a little as she walked forward and tossed a white rose into the hole, onto her father's casket. When she turned and stepped away, she looked off to the distance. West of here was Saddleback Ranch, their home for as long as she could remember. It had been handed down for three generations now.

Straightening her shoulders and looking off to the distance, she knew in her heart that she'd do anything-anything—to keep it. To keep her and her sisters together. On their land. Like her father and mother would have wanted her to do.

After shaking the hands of and hugging almost

everyone in the small three-thousand-person strong community, she stood outside her truck talking briefly with Grant Holton Sr., her father's lawyer and one of his best friends. Mr. Holton was tall and very broad chested. She'd heard once that he and her father had played football together.

She looked over as Dr. Graham and his son, Chase, walked up to them. Dr. Graham had been the ranch's veterinarian. Every animal on her land was healthy thanks to the older man who walked forward and shook her hand with a firm grip. Chase had been a year ahead of her in school. They'd grown up together and had even gone to a couple dances together in high school and had shared a few stolen kisses behind the bleachers. But then he'd graduated, and she'd seen less and less of him.

Chase was tall like his father. It looked like he'd tried to grease back his bushy mass of black hair for the ceremony. She'd always loved pushing her hands into his thick hair. His dark brown eyes stared at her with sincere concern and grief, much like his fathers did now.

"Lauren." Dr. Graham shook her hand, then Mr. Holton's.

Mr. Holton nodded, then turned towards her. "I know this isn't the time to think about your future or the ranch's future, but maybe we can meet tomorrow. Just the three of us. There are a few details I need to go over with you."

At that moment, the realization hit her—she was the head of the house. She was now in charge of a thousand-acre ranch. In charge of her sisters. In charge of the cattle, the horses, everything. She must have paled a little because Chase stepped forward and took her elbow. "Are you okay?" he whispered.

She wanted to shove his arm away and scream. "No! I'm not okay, you idiot. Everything is ruined! I have no family left." But instead, she nodded and swayed a little, causing him to move his other arm around her waist. "Dad," Chase said, looking towards his father.

"Quite right, we apologize." The older man cleared his throat, looking towards his friend.

"No," Lauren blinked. If she wanted to keep the three of them on her family's land, she would just have to step up a little more. Remember, she told herself, keep your sisters together and do whatever it takes to stay on your family's land. "If you want, I'm heading back to the house now. We can meet in say"—she looked at her watch as Chase dropped his arm— "an hour?"

Dr. Graham and Mr. Holton nodded their heads in unison. She could see the questions in their eyes. Lauren turned when she spotted her sisters walking towards her. She walked stiffly around to the driver's side of her truck, her shoulders square. As they drove away in silence, she looked back and saw the three men standing there. A shiver rolled down her back and she knew at that moment that everything was going to change.

The drive to the ranch wasn't a long one. It sat almost ten miles outside of town, but the roads were always empty, and the highway stretched in a straight line. When they passed the old iron gate with Saddleback Ranch overhead, she felt a little peace settle in her bones. There, in the distance, stood the three-story house she'd always known and loved. It had taken some bangs in its time. The tornado that had claimed their mother had torn the roof right off the massive place. The old red barn had been flattened back then as well. They'd lost a dozen horses and two of the farmhand houses. Thank goodness her father and the men had been in the hills that day, or they might have been caught up in the storm as well. But the barn and farmhands' houses had been rebuilt. The house had gotten a shiny new roof, along with a new paint job and some new windows panes to replace the ones that had blown out. After her father replaced the storm cellar's door, no one talked about that day anymore.

Lauren stopped the truck in front of the barn, and Haley jumped out and ran through the massive doors. Alex turned and looked at Lauren.

"Don't worry. I'll go talk to her." Lauren patted her sister's thigh and got out of the truck. Dingo, the family dog, an Australian shepherd mix, rushed up to Lauren and jumped on her dress. "No, down." She pushed the dog off, but she followed her into the dark barn.

Outside, the sun had warmed her, but here in the darkness of the barn, the coolness seeped into her bones. She rubbed her arms with her hands as she walked forward to climb the old stairs that led to the second floor, where she knew her sister would be.

The loft was huge, taking up three-quarters of the barn, but Lauren knew Haley's hiding places and walked right to her sister. Haley was stretched out on the soft hay, her best Sunday dress fanned out around her. She was face down and crying like there was no tomorrow. Lauren walked over and sat next to her. She pulled her into her arms and cried with her.

Less than an hour later, Lauren had changed into her work clothes and stood at the door to greet Mr. Holton, Dr. Graham, and, to her surprise, Chase. The four of them walked into her father's large office and she shut the glass doors behind her. Taking a large breath, she turned to face the room.

"Please, have a seat." She motioned for the three men to sit as she walked around her father's massive desk and sat in his soft leather chair. She'd done it a hundred times, but this time it felt different.

"Your father was a great man," Mr. Holton started. "He was our best friend." He looked at Dr. Graham, and the other man nodded his head in agreement. "We could postpone this meeting for—"

"No, please." Lauren straightened her shoulders.

"Very well." Mr. Holton pulled out a file from his briefcase. "As you know, I am your father's lawyer. John, here"—he nodded to Dr. Graham— "well, he has a stake in what we need to discuss. That's why I invited him along."

"Continue," Lauren said when she thought Mr. Holton had lost his nerve. She knew it was bad news; she could see it clearly on both man's faces.

"Well, after that day"—Mr. Holton cleared his throat and shifted in his seat— "after we lost your mother, Richard took out some loans."

"Mr. Holton how much did my father owe the bank?" She wanted the bottom line. Holding her breath, she waited.

"Well, that's the tricky part. You see, Richard didn't trust in banks all that much." The two older men looked between themselves. "Maybe this will explain it better." He set the file on the desk in front of her.

She opened the file with shaky fingers. There, in her father's handwriting, was her future.

I, Richard West, being of sound body and mind, do

solemnly promise to pay back the total sum of $100,000.00 to Johnathan Graham Sr. and Grant Holton II. If anything should happen to me, the proceeds of my ranch, Saddleback Ranch, would go to both men in equal amounts until paid back in full. They would have a say in the running of the ranch until the said amount was paid in full.

It had been dated and signed by her father, John Graham, and Grant Holton Sr. over ten years ago.

"I understand your concerns." She looked up from the paper. "As head of the house now, I will fulfill my father's obligations."

"Well, that's all well and good." Dr. Graham smiled. "But, well, we had an understanding between the three of us. If anything happened to him and we saw that you three or the ranch was in any jeopardy, we'd step in and run this place until we saw fit."

Lauren listened as the men told her the scheme the three of them—her father, Mr. Holton and Dr. Graham— had come up with ten years ago in case anything like this should happen. How they'd take over the running of the land, the handling of the finances, even deciding how to deal with her and her sisters. She was being pushed out before she'd even had the chance to try and run things her way. She'd practically raised her sisters, and now these two men wanted to take control of everything, even her. Her heart sank upon hearing this news. She asked for some time to think about it and the men apologized and quickly excused themselves.

After the older men had driven away, Chase stayed behind and offered her another option. The next day Lauren stood in front of the courthouse in Tyler, wearing her Sunday best. She knew her life would never be the same again after that day.

Seven years later…

Chase stood in the middle of the street and took a deep breath. He was finally home. It wasn't that he'd been avoiding the place, or that he hadn't had the will to return, but life had led him down a twisted path. He was happy that he'd finally ended up back here, at least for now. A car horn honked at him, and he waved and moved from the center of the road. Walking up the stone steps to his father's building, he realized that the old green place had never looked better. He knew the money he'd been sending home over the last nine years had helped with fixing up the clinic.

When he opened the front door, the bell above the door chimed and he smiled.

"Morning, how can I—" Cheryl, his father's receptionist, stood slowly. "Son of a…"

"Now, Cheryl, you know you're not supposed to say that around here." He walked forward and received her welcome hug. The woman almost engulfed him, but he smiled and took the beating as she patted his back hard. Her arms were like vices, but her front was soft, and she smelled just like he remembered, like chocolate and wet puppies. The odd mix of aromas had always warmed his spirits.

"What are you doing back in town?" she asked. She gasped. "Does your father know?" She looked toward the back room.

He shook his head. "I wanted to surprise him." He smiled.

Her smile slipped a little. "Well, you sure will." Then she bit her bottom lip and he knew something was up.

"Spill." He took her shoulders before she could turn away.

"What?" She tried to look innocent.

"Cheryl, how long have I known you?"

She smiled. "Going on twenty-eight years next June." He smiled. Cheryl always did remember his birthday.

"And in all that time, I've come to know that when you bite your bottom lip, you have something you're trying to hide. So..."—he motioned with his hand— "spill."

She crossed her arms over her chest. "Fine. It's just your father's health. I know he hasn't mentioned it over the phone to you."

"What about it?" Chase began to get worried and felt like rushing to the back room to check up on his dad. Cheryl had never mentioned anything personal about his father's health in their conversations. Neither had his father.

"Well, he injured his leg a while back." She twisted her shirtfront.

"And?" He waited.

"And, well, he's walking with a cane now," she blurted out, just as his father walked through the back door.

"Thank you, Cheryl. That will be enough out of you." His father smiled. Sure enough, his father was leaning on a black cane. "Well, boy?" He held out his arm. "Don't make me hobble over to you for that hug."

Chase rushed across the room and gave his old man a bear hug like he always had, noticing that his father was not only skinnier but felt frailer. He had a million questions he wanted to ask but knew his father wouldn't answer until he was good and ready.

"Come on back here, boy. Tell me what you've been up to." His father started walking towards the back and Chase watched him hobble. Then his father turned. "Are you back to stay?"

"Yes," Chase said absentmindedly. He hadn't meant to stay, had he?

"Good." His father turned into his office and took a seat, setting the cane down beside him. Chase sat in the chair across from him, waiting.

"Well, I suppose I should tell you, you couldn't have come home at a better time. I'm retiring."

"What?" Chase sat up. His father raised his hands, holding off the million questions he had.

"Yes, at the end of the year. I've been kicked one too many times." His father smiled. "This old body doesn't want to work like it used to. I was going to give you a call later this month."

"Dad?" He looked at him.

"I know, I know. I told you I'd never retire, but..." he looked down at his leg. "The doctors are telling me I have to be off this damned leg for six hours a day. Six! You and I both know that in this line of work you'd be lucky to sit for five minutes a day."

Chase smiled. "I guess it's a good thing I'm home, then."

His father smiled and nodded his head. "What do you say we go grab some lunch? I'm buying."

Fairplay, Texas, had one place to sit and eat. Mama's Diner, a huge brown barn that had been turned into a restaurant, had been the best place to eat in two counties since as far back as Chase could remember. Even now the place looked new and smelled like greasy burgers.

His father took his usual booth. It almost made Chase laugh, knowing the man never sat in a different spot. Even if someone was in it, he'd stand and wait until the table was cleared. There were new menus and he took his time looking over the list of new items.

"How are you today, beautiful?" his father asked the waitress when she stopped by.

Chase looked up and stared into the most beautiful green eyes he'd ever seen. Her hair was longer than before, and her dark curls hung just below the most perfect breasts he'd ever had the pleasure of being up against. She was tall and limber and he could remember the softness of every curve he'd been allowed to feel. She looked down at him like he was in her way and he started coughing. He couldn't explain how it happened, but he was choking on air. Nothing was getting through to his lungs or to his brain. Finally, she smacked his back hard, and he took a deep breath. He stood and grabbed Lauren's arm and demanded in a low voice, "What the hell are you doing working here?"

This is a work of fiction. Names, characters, places, and incidents are either the product of the author's imagination or are used fictitiously, and any resemblance to actual persons, living or dead, business establishments, events, or locales is entirely coincidental.

PRINT ISBN: 978-1-942896-60-9

DIGITAL ISBN: 978-1-942896-03-6

Copyeditor: Erica Ellis – inkdeepediting.com

Missy's Moment

Breaking Travis

Roping Ryan

Wild Bride

Corey's Catch

Tessa's Turn

The Grayton Series

Last Resort

Someday Beach

Rip Current

In Too Deep

Swept Away

High Tide

Lucky Series

Unlucky In Love

Sweet Resolve

Best of Luck

A Little Luck

Silver Cove Series

Silver Lining

French Kiss

Happy Accident

Hidden Charm

A Silver Cove Christmas

Entangled Series – Paranormal Romance

The Awakening

The Beckoning

The Ascension

Haven, Montana Series

Closer to You

Never Let Go

Holding On

Pride Oregon Series

A Dash of Love

My Kind of Love

Season of Love

Tis the Season

Dare to Love

Where I Belong

Wildflowers Series

Summer Nights

Summer Heat

Stand Alone Books

Twisted Rock

For a complete list of books:

http://JillSanders.com

ABOUT THE AUTHOR

Jill Sanders is a New York Times, USA Today, and international bestselling author of Sweet Contemporary Romance, Romantic Suspense, Western Romance, and Paranormal Romance novels. With over 55 books in eleven series, translations into several different languages, and audiobooks there's plenty to choose from. Look for Jill's bestselling stories wherever romance books are sold or visit her at jillsanders.com

Jill comes from a large family with six siblings, including an identical twin. She was raised in the Pacific Northwest and later relocated to Colorado for college and a successful IT career before discovering her talent for writing sweet and sexy page-turners. After Colorado, she decided to move south, living in Texas and now making her home along the Emerald Coast of Florida. You will find that the settings of several of her series are inspired by her time spent living in these areas. She has two sons and off-set the testosterone in her house by adopting three furry little ladies that provide her company while she's locked in her writing cave. She enjoys heading to the beach, hiking, swimming, wine-tasting, and pickleball with her husband, and of course writing. If you have read any of her books, you may also notice that there is a love of food, especially sweets! She has been blamed for a few added pounds by her assistant, editor, and fans... donuts or pie anyone?

facebook.com/JillSandersBooks

twitter.com/JillMSanders

bookbub.com/authors/jill-sanders